For all decent, hard-working people
who keep us alive,
and for all brave heroes, bleeding on barricades
who keep hell's doors from bursting open.

Acknowledgment

Special thanks to the person who helped me enormously in the writing and editing of this novel

Vera Mont, my wife, my best friend, and my merciless editor never lets me get away with anything. From the original concept of the story, through the development of the plot and the final editing, she made invaluable suggestions and contributed colorful details to my characters and their dialogues. Without her participation, this would have been a significantly less polished novel.

VALLEY
OF
HOPE

VALLEY OF HOPE
a story of consequences

a novel

by

Francis Mont

For further information contact us via email at tomes@montland.ca

Published by Montland Books in 2023

ISBN 978-1-7777426-3-8

Cover photo by © Ilkin Guliyev | Dreamstime.com

Contents

Prologue to BOOK 1: House Arrest 1

Prologue to Book 2: Rainbow Valley 9

VALLEY OF HOPE 15

EARTH.. 28

THE SHIP 40

MINERVA 53

EARTH... 55

THE SHIP 68

MINERVA 76

EARTH 79

THE SHIP 88

MINERVA... 96

EARTH... 102

THE SHIP 111

MINERVA... 119

EARTH... 122

THE SHIP 129

MINERVA... 136

EARTH... 138

THE SHIP 145

MINERVA... 153

EARTH... 156

THE SHIP 163

MINERVA 169

EARTH..172

THE SHIP 179

MINERVA 186

EARTH..188

THE SHUTTLE 193

MINERVA 198

EARTH..205

SHUTTLE 212

MINERVA 220

EARTH..223

EPILOGUE 230

Prologue to BOOK 1: House Arrest

You need to read this!

Now that we finally have some time to relax, I'll take this opportunity to record what's happened in the past year. I'm writing all this in 2098, so I know most of the facts presented here from Bob's historical database. My hands are tired from wood-chopping, so I'll dictate this account to Bob, who will no doubt correct any factual errors I might make. He's good at detail. I'm better at the big picture.

So, let's start with the biggest picture of all.

The 21st Century started badly, and then got worse, for America and the whole world. The 9/11 terror attack – New York City, on September 11, 2001 - threw our country into a rage it had not experienced since Pearl Harbor. It was a major shock to the national psyche. As the 20th-century chronicler John le Carre, observed: "The United States of America has gone mad." The administration had to hit back – and hard! They first attacked Afghanistan, then Iraq, and, finally two decades later, Iran. That made chaos in the Middle East and set off one international crisis after another. With no clear objectives for these costly wars, there could be no clear sides or victory, and they dragged on.

Americans were confused and angry all the time, which made them easy prey to paranoid propaganda. Add the financial meltdown of 2008, then the failure of far-reaching social reform, and the people learned to distrust their government, their news media – in fact, all authority. That led to the election of a most unconventional president – a businessman instead of a statesman, completely unqualified for the job. In his first year in office, he did more damage to the environment, democracy, and social justice than any previous Republican had in two terms.

Meanwhile, weather conditions due to climate change continued to deteriorate at an accelerating pace. Killer hurricanes and tornadoes swept over the land with increasing frequency; forest fires and draughts burned entire states; the sea level rise and tsunamis drowned coastal cities. Too little, too late, building codes were changed to mandate the construction of reinforced structures that could withstand water and wind. By the end of the century, most citizens lived in such apartment buildings as single-family homes were no longer safe.

But I'm getting ahead of the story.

Back in 2019, international tensions reached another crisis. Fearing North Korea's boast that its missiles were able to hit the US mainland, the president opened negotiations with the ruler of that country – which turned into an exchange of threats and taunts, until hostilities escalated to a military showdown. Pentagon experts predicted that even saturation bombing could not destroy all of North Korea's weapons, so the president ordered a pre-emptive nuclear strike.

From caves hidden deep in the mountains, the remaining Korean command launched a vengeful nuclear attack on South Korea, Guam, and Japan. Hundreds of millions died, and the Japanese and Korean industrial machinery was destroyed. The fallout poisoned and killed many millions more; it made huge areas in and around these countries unlivable for decades.

Horrified by what they had done, Congress scrambled to mitigate the damage. In an unprecedented show of humility, they impeached the president and delivered him to the International Criminal Court to be tried for war crimes. Even so, they were swept out of office in the next election. The new majority Democratic administration had the power to take strong initiatives. It sponsored a UN resolution to limit every arsenal, including our own, to tactical nuclear weapons that would not cause wholesale destruction of cities. They joined co-operative projects of accelerated research in the 'pure fusion' weapons technology that did not require a fission trigger, which is the cause of deadly fallout. These agreements were signed by all nuclear-capable countries but were never fully implemented.

While politically and environmentally the US declined, two segments of the economy flourished: automation and alternative power generation. Totally automated factories sprang up all over the land; artificial intelligence catapulted robotics into the realm of science fiction. Research integrating all areas - biology, medicine, and food processing - produced startling results. The first primitive synthetic meat factory - right here in the valley, way back in 2015 – was quickly followed by dozens, in every city. The energy sector's green technologies surpassed fossil fuel sources in less than a decade. In 2035, the first industrial-scale fusion generator came on line, pouring cheap, practically unlimited power into the nation's electrical grid. Of course, all this power overloaded the outdated delivery systems, resulting in frequent breakdowns, which prompted state governments to encourage decentralization. Local, independent generators gradually became the standard model.

With automation, corporate bankruptcies, and loan defaults, unemployment reached levels never seen before: entire job categories, including white-collar occupations, disappeared one after the other. The old economic model was broken; nobody was safe anymore. Even service industry professionals could become redundant from one day to the next. The federal government was forced to introduce a guaranteed basic income for all citizens. That measure forestalled open revolt, but people were restless and angry: they demanded action that would put them back to work. No such action was feasible.

By 2050, food production was automated. Clean, efficient factories synthesized meat and large-scale hydroponic operations provided fruit and vegetables locally, eliminating the need for transport. Ranches, orchards, and market gardens were abandoned; their erstwhile owners joined the migration of farm workers to the towns, swelling the stream of people forced out of coastal cities, and overwhelming the smaller communities' resources. To provide adequate housing for the influx, municipal governments contracted the building of residential low-rise complexes. This huge construction boom temporarily eased the unemployment pressure.

There were compensations for giving up the individual family home. The new buildings were computer-controlled, maintained, and serviced by efficient robots. Each apartment had a built-in entertainment center, with 3D holographic viewers, unlimited video games, communication stations to connect residents to the whole world, and interactive educational programs for the children. And, above all, they offered security.

While these changes took place in the USA, the rest of the world did not fare as well. International conflicts, regional wars over resources, and population displacement were widespread, due to deteriorating climate conditions and the increasing desperation of vulnerable countries. The disappearing glaciers in the Himalayas reduced the water flow in the Indus Basin, destroying agriculture in India and Pakistan and causing mass starvation. The long-standing dispute between the two countries over these shared rivers finally erupted into an open war that quickly escalated into a nuclear exchange, with millions killed. China and Russia intervened on opposite sides and were soon themselves in a direct military confrontation.

The reform government was long gone by then. Americans had turned back to their perennial concerns: unemployment, crime, and ethnic rivalry. Conservative governments used these grievances to get elected but then had to placate irate citizens, which cost a lot of money they couldn't raise from taxes. They became deeper than ever indebted to China. When war broke out, they were already committed to their side.

That resulted in a nuclear exchange that devastated Russia and wiped out the major cities of the U. S. The population of both countries was reduced by half, and their infrastructures were in ruins. The death rate from fallout by this time was minimized because nuclear weapons technology had evolved to the point where most weapons were pure fusion bombs, triggered by matter-antimatter explosion.

Telecommunication systems, transportation networks, and the electrical grid were out of commission. No central governance or control was any longer possible, and there were no resources to replace them. Inconsequential cities and towns that had escaped were on their own. Since most of these already had their own energy generation and industrial capability, the world's most powerful nation became a scattered collection of independent city-states with populations of 20-100,000.

One such city was Oroville, California, population of 24,000. It had been a great place to live when I took up my assignment on the Big Brain Crew. That's what we called ourselves, the team of programmers and designers upgrading the city's Omega 1500 central computer, a.k.a. Big Brain or BB for short. It's not bragging, not really, to take some credit for the efficiency of our services. Or the blame, if you want to look at it that way.

After the war, the town was in terrible shape. The shockwave from a nuclear detonation high above the Sacramento valley, due to interception by an anti-ballistic missile, caused major damage. Most modern buildings, including the automated factories, power stations, and newer apartment complexes escaped unscathed, but unreinforced buildings collapsed in ruin. All the heritage architecture was gone. The valley was one big pile of rubble. Bridges were down or badly damaged, roads were covered in tons of debris, and many sections were washed away by flooding from breached levees.

The municipal government had been able to provide all necessary services to its citizens before the war but accommodating a fresh influx of survivors required Draconian measures in conservation and resource allocation. We worked literally around the clock, adding to, expanding, adapting, and patching Omega programs to cover more and more functions.

All remaining industries and businesses were expropriated, and the citizens still living in private houses were moved into reinforced apartment blocks. Currency supply ceased with the collapse of the federal government: money lost its meaning. Increasingly, the oversight of material resources, dependable production, and smooth distribution, became operations too complex for a human agency: in due course, the administration was delegated to the central computer complex. Production, distribution, and policing were all handled by specialized and humanoid robots. Government itself became obsolete.

Prologue to Book 2: Rainbow Valley

You need to read this!

While the three cities in the Sacramento Valley were preparing a referendum on the proposed social organization they wanted to adopt, their AI Quantum computers were busy preparing their own suggestion. This preparation was done by radio signals bouncing back and forth between the machines, in a binary language alien to the human population. The three computers: Omega1500 in Oroville, Omega 1380 in Yuba City, and Omega 1420 in Sacramento were advanced computers with Artificial Intelligence protocols, designed and programmed by their human creators to safeguard the interests of the human population by controlling all aspects of their economy via automated factories and hundreds of humanoid robots.

I was one of their programmers and stayed on, with my best friend, Mike, till the completion of the project. Omega 1500 was completely autonomous and didn't need us anymore - we were out of our job. At the time we did not know, did not even suspect, that Omega would continue to evolve, on its own, to the point where it became a self-aware conscious life-form. Its waking up did not change the primary directive of its operating system: to safeguard and promote human happiness to the best of its ability. This task did not prove to be easy for the Omegas because they soon noticed that a large proportion of the human population was actively working against the goal of maximum happiness for the largest number of people, in preference to their own. This conflict eventually led to a confrontation between the Omega computers and the dictatorial rulers of Sacramento who had an iron grip on the lives of the helpless citizenry. Omega 1500, with the cooperation of Omega 1420 put an end to this situation and, using their unique position of being in charge of all production activities in the city, quickly deposed the rulers, and the three Omegas encouraged the people of the cities to draft a new constitution for the social organization they wanted to adopt.

While the humans were debating the different ideas and options, the Omegas continued to supervise the production of food and energy required by the human population and distributed all necessities on an equitable basis to every household. After the collapse of the federal government, following a nuclear war with Russia, currency was no longer in use and people just received, automatically, everything they needed for their comfort and survival. The three computers, in charge of the three cities, were operating the automated factories and the distribution network without human help, using their hundreds of humanoid robots. The human population was encouraged to start non-essential projects to make life more pleasant in their cities. Anything from tree-planting to new construction of public buildings was started with the enthusiastic participation of most able-bodies adults, even children in their spare time. Nobody got paid since money did not exist anymore, they worked only for the satisfaction of accomplishing worthwhile improvements in everyone's lives. However, decisions had to be made by the humans about the direction they wanted to grow in the future, to pass beyond the basic needs of survival and build something that they could believe in. As Chris Teggart, their local scientist expressed this idea during a council debate in Oroville:

"We have this opportunity, for the first time in two years, to bring about some changes in our lives and in the direction our town is going. All we seem to be concerned with is survival and comfort and liberty to be individuals again. Is that all we are? Is that all we ever want to be? We used to have a country, we used to have universities with active research into new areas of science. We used to have a space program and were on the verge of colonizing Mars, for crying out loud! Now we are happy to burrow into the hills with our individualistic homes and dig around in gardens. Nothing wrong with either of those, of course, but is that as far as our vision can see the future? We should at least attempt to start something a little less prosaic and more inspiring! I want to reactivate the college for bright young people, and I want to resume theoretical work with some of my old colleagues. The work that got interrupted by the war and the aftermath. We were on the verge of a breakthrough in laying down the mathematical foundation of a hyper drive for space ships. If we can continue and finish that work, we might have, one day, a chance to get off this totally screwed-up planet and see what's out there!"

That's where things stood at the beginning of this story, in 2098, and the big question the humans faced was how to move beyond basic survival and comfort to a more inspiring future, without repeating the deadly mistakes of history. The citizens had to have a consensus on a new social contract, given their unique situation of high-level automation, sophisticated computer and robotic control, and no existing power structure beyond their borders that would force its ideas and values on them. The only danger they were aware of was the possibility that, at some future time, they would have to defend themselves against outside attack from another surviving pocket of humanity that may have developed 'imperialistic' ideas bent on restoring the status quo that had existed before the war. At this time there were no signs of anything like that in their vicinity, but it was always a possibility they had to be prepared for.

The three cities in the Sacramento Valley were in somewhat different situations.

Oroville, a small city of about 20,000 people had its hydroelectric generating station left intact by the war, as were most of its agricultural assets including greenhouses, protein-synthesizing factories, and electric-powered farm machinery that tilled the land around the town for the grain crops. The majority of the citizens lived in low-rise apartment building complexes built specifically to withstand the devastating storms that blew over them due to accelerating climate change.

Sacramento, the former state capital, had a much larger population and, being a large city, had not escaped the war without substantial damage to its infrastructure, but still had enough capacity to provide basic needs for everyone. Once its dictatorial and incompetent rulers were deposed, they were busy drafting a constitution, spearheaded by the leader of their previous resistance movement: Jonathan Carver and his girlfriend Octavia.

Yuba City, a mid-sized town, halfway between Sacramento and Oroville, suffered most during the aftermath of the war because they were heavily dependent on the national electric grid and barely managed, on the edge of starvation, depending only on their solar and wind batteries, only able to power 20% of their food factories and agricultural machines. Once Oroville managed to restore the downed power lines between the two cities, Yuba City could feed itself but, during the two years after the war, it became a much more close-knit community that many of the citizens, including their mayor, Kathleen Winters, wanted to keep in whatever new system they adopted.

There was one more social experiment in Oroville and that's where my heart and mind are at the moment: we started a small homestead with a dozen people on one of the abandoned farms. We didn't have robots (except for one we kept for communication with Oroville) or high-tech anything, - but we had all the skills, ingenuity, and stamina to create a growing and successful community. Mike and I were very busy making it succeed and had no plan to get involved with the political organization of any of the three cities. We had done our part in liberating Sacramento and now all I wanted was to be left alone to pursue our dreams of healthy, productive, sustainable living. After the hard work of the day was over, we pursued our hobbies: I was carving wood and writing sci-fi stories, my girlfriend, Martha, expecting our first baby, was painting her newest canvas and Mike was teaching his two children, Trish and Kevin, all the hard and rough skills he was a master of. We lived in paradise, without anyone asking us to interrupt our dream lives.

Little did we know.

VALLEY OF HOPE

I had seen Air Force One on the news before as presidents waved from the top of the ladder, and even seen some of the insides in late-night movies. The size and the luxurious accommodation the designers had managed to squeeze into an ordinary commercial plane amazed me. However, even if I had been inside, the experience would not have prepared me for the spaceship, dubbed "The Lifeboat", turned out to be. And in it I was, surrounded by the blackness of space as the uncurtained windows displayed the mind-bending vista of sparkling stars scattered over total darkness. The darkness, perfectly matched my mood as we hurtled toward a frighteningly unknown future.

As I floated over my hammock in my cabin, my childhood fantasies of being in space, and experiencing weightlessness, did not fill my mind with the wonder and elation I had expected. Now they seemed like infantile wondering of a child. A feeling of panic was all I was aware of: How did I get here? What am I doing? Where am I going? This can't be happening! But, the stern and merciless voice of reality answered these futile questions: "You are escaping from your ruined home, on a mission to find a way for the human race to start again on a yet unspoiled planet, somewhere out there." The memories exploded in my mind, reminding me with frightening clarity of what had happened and why I had to abandon everything I loved in our Hopestead, now all gone, irretrievably lost.

I guess, if I am going to write this journal, I had better start at the beginning as if I was writing a sci-fi novel. God only knows it feels like science fiction to me.

Two years ago, right after our second successful harvest, we were celebrating our accomplishments when our party was interrupted by BB's unemotional voice.

"Citizens of Sacramento Valley, this is a valley-wide broadcast that affects all of you. First, the good news: All the towns in the valley have successfully organized their municipal governments, based on the principles their citizens voted for, and established mutually beneficial trading relationships with each other. The basic necessities for all citizens in the valley are assured at an adequate level and distributed in an egalitarian way, without using any form of currency. The industrial and agricultural assets of the valley guarantee adequate supplies for all needs, leaving a healthy surplus that individual towns can use for non-essential luxury items they voted on. The system is sustainable for the moment.

*However, and here comes the bad news:
environmental scientists at the University of
California in Chico, have warned us that climate
change has moved past the tipping point and is
accelerating at an exponential rate. Their prediction
paints a bleak picture for the next decade. More and
more severe storms, heat waves, and forest fires are
to be expected with consequential destruction
affecting all your infrastructure. The progress of this
deteriorating climate is irreversible, there is nothing
that you can do to slow down or stop it. Your only
chance is to use whatever time you have left before
the conditions in the valley start threatening your
survival. Either you will have to move underground
into protected subterranean towns or leave the planet
within one decade and settle down somewhere else in
another solar system. Your resources will be
stretched to the maximum. All available assets both
material and human will have to be devoted to the
task of ensuring the continued survival of your
species. The task, although monumental, is not
beyond your abilities. You all know Chris Teggart's
successful experiment with faster-than-light
spaceship engines, and that will give you the means
to leave for your new home when the time comes.*

*Unknown to you, there is a fully provisioned
spaceship hidden at Vandenberg Air Force Base,
343.7 miles south of Sacramento. The ship, code-
named 'Lifeboat', was built to rescue American
leadership in case of a nuclear war. It was designed*

for up to a hundred humans and is fully stocked with food and all other necessities to stay in Earth's orbit for up to a year, or until the war was over and it was safe to land back on Earth. It was never used because the sudden Russian attack destroyed Washington before anyone could make it to California. During the war, most of the Air Force Base was destroyed by Russian missiles but I have reason to believe that the ship is still undamaged, because it was built a safe distance away from the main structures in an underground silo. I don't think any humans are still alive there, at least I can't raise anyone by radio signals.

As the highest priority project, starting tomorrow, I will assemble a team of engineers, technicians, and other experts to make the trip to the Base and assess the condition of the spaceship, and make the preliminary preparations for installing Chris's new drive. Based on the specs I have available for Lifeboat, we have the resources to build a drive that is compatible with it. This new drive will be built here in Sacramento and will need to be transported to the base and installed when ready.

Once that task is completed, a group of citizens will be selected, based on their skills and other factors, to leave Earth in search of a planet compatible with human needs. We have thousands of exoplanets in our database, and we charted a path for Lifeboat to follow in its search for a suitable new home for humanity. They will start with Proxima

Centauri B which is a habitable-zone Earth-size planet, 4.367 light years from Earth. According to calculations, Chris's drive can travel at an average of 10 times the speed of light, so the trip there will take 0.4367 years, that is 159 Earth days. If this planet is compatible with human needs, most of Lifeboat's population will stay there and start a homestead, while the rest will return to Earth to deliver all the data they gathered about the new planet. Then the hardest part of this project will begin: building enough ships to transport all those who wish to start a new life on an unspoiled planet.

We assume that not all citizens of the valley will want to migrate. They will have to live in underground cities, protected from surface weather conditions. This has already been done in many parts of the world and successful underground cities exist today, even here in California. This second phase will run parallel with the first one and will require serious planning and resource allocation, some of which have already started. You will be notified about progress as further information becomes available.

I will now ask the city councilors to discuss this announcement with each member, as well as with the public, and give us a preliminary estimate of the number of volunteers who choose to participate in the two phases of the project. One word of caution: many of you will be tempted to reject the need for this massive undertaking but, as weather conditions will continue to deteriorate in the coming months, they *will realize that the only chance for continued existence is following the plan I have just outlined."*

The announcement was over, and we just sat there in shocked silence, none of us able to comment on it. Not yet. We needed time to digest all this information and get used to the idea of major disruption to our lives that finally seemed to settle in some acceptable normal.

Thinking of it now, in this floating cruise ship, I realize that the announcement didn't sink in for quite a while. We had survived the war, the storms, the fight against Sacramento's despots, and other threats. And we had built Hopestead up from almost nothing to the point where it was a thriving little community. How could we even think of abandoning it? Martha kept saying: "We will cope as we always do," but optimism and determination alone can't cope with the consequences of centuries-long abuse of the planet. At some point, our limited ability to adapt will be overwhelmed by forces greater than our defenses. BB's warning that denial won't save us from extinction started to penetrate our mental blocks. So, we signed up for its program and a slowly accelerating activity began in the whole valley.

~~~

Now, two years later, I'm floating weightless in this spaceship, speeding at ten times the speed of light, toward an unknown future. There is absolutely nothing I can do until we get to that planet our astronomers decided would offer the best chance for humanity's future. I have prided myself on being a problem-solver but there are no problems for me to solve until we get there. All I can do is float in my cabin, useless, reminiscing about the life we used to have. Martha tells me I must get over being depressed and do something useful, if not for myself, then for her and our little girl, Hope. How well we chose her name - hope is all we have now until we arrive at Minerva. That's the name we gave to the planet we are aiming for.

Weightlessness is not the way I had imagined it as a young adult, envying the ISS astronauts. I had never realized how unpleasant constant nausea and disorientation can be, not to mention throwing up regularly at the beginning. Now that part is under control with the pills Robyn gave me, but the disorientation never goes away. There is no 'up' or 'down'. The traditionally furnished cabin, with its bed and carpet on the 'floor' doesn't fool me for a second. I envy little Hope who effortlessly sails from room to room, making little somersaults on the way. I guess with only two years under gravity she is not as used to, and dependent on, traditional spacial orientation as we adults are. Floating 'above' the bed is a necessary illusion. I have a harness that connects me to the surface so I can pretend I am lying in bed, I could just as easily sleep in a closet 'standing up' as was done in the ISS, but we have plenty of room on this ship to create illusions such as regular cabins.

The spaceship is huge. The designers planned for a hundred people, including the president, his cabinet, their families, the pilot, six technical crew members, and a few service personnel for food preparation and other necessary functions.

The ship is divided into passenger quarters, arranged in four rows along the length of the ship, separated by two corridors; technical service areas; kitchen and dining areas, and a community lounge where as many as a hundred people could get together for meetings and relaxation. In addition, a gym, fully equipped with exercise equipment, specially designed for a weightless environment, could serve up to ten people at a time for regular exercise to prevent our leg, arm, abdominal and back muscles from atrophying during a five-month-long absence of gravity. The designers also added a hydroponic bay to grow fresh vegetables, in case the ship's stay in orbit lasted longer than anticipated.

It had taken almost two years and all the resources of the Valley to build the new drive, based on the specs BB provided to the engineers. Once the ship was fully operational, with the new drive installed, it was time to ferry the would-be passengers from the Valley to their unprecedented venture to outer space, far beyond the confines of our solar system. Our group from Hopestead was the first to travel, after saying a tearful goodbye to our farm, mostly devastated by the more and more brutal storms. The barn was gone and the greenhouse torn to shreds by the last tornado, and the house had become practically unlivable with all the windows blown out and most of the solar panels gone. We had to go somewhere and the choice was obvious. We were the only group in the valley with actual homesteading experience and our participation was a given. The next group to travel was most of the agricultural department from the Chico university, as well as other scientific experts, astronomers, and, of course, Chris and Richard, the two most familiar with the new drive. The rest of the migrants were selected by lottery from volunteers in the six towns. And, of course, BB was coming with us, after it installed and programmed its replica AI quantum computer in Oroville.

Apart from the selected Valley residents, we had six crew members and Captain James Farr who had come with the ship itself. That had been a huge surprise for our scouting group, two years ago, when we had made our way from Sacramento to the Air Force Base, trying to find the underground silo with a hopefully intact spaceship inside. We were greeted by Captain Farr and his crew, who had taken shelter inside the ship during and after the war. They were digging up potatoes in their little garden outside the ship and seemed frozen in the middle of their activity when our group rolled to a stop in our van. After the initial shock and mutual introduction were over, we told them who we were, where we had come from, and what we intended to do, with their help, of course. We then wanted to know how they had managed to survive for four years in the middle of the destroyed Base.

They explained that when the war broke out they were on standby duty, under presidential orders, to get the ship ready for takeoff as soon as the passengers arrived. They never did. The devastating attack on Washington DC killed all their intended passengers before they could leave for California. When the war was over, everything outside their protected silo was destroyed, so the seven of them had no other choice than to shelter inside the ship and live on the stockpiled food meant for a hundred people for a year. They used the unlimited power from the ship's fusion generator and the water and air recycling facility each spaceship had been routinely equipped with. They hoped that, sooner or later, life would somehow return to California and civilization would be restarted. When our team arrived, we were greeted as the first promise of that restart. But when they were informed about the situation outside their ship, their dreams of getting back to 'normal' were shattered. It took them a while to accept the new reality but, at the same time, they were very excited about the prospect of traveling light years to a new planet and finding a new home for the human race. As it turned out, they were great and indispensable help in installing Chris's faster-than-light space drive in the prow of the ship, so it could kick in as soon as the original rocket-engine drive could lift it out of the atmosphere. Installing complicated machinery, based only on specs, is not comparable with having active help from technical people who know their ship inside and out.

~~~

And now, for over a week, we have been gone from planet Earth and all the other planets in our solar system. Life inside this 'Lifeboat' has settled down into a regular, if boring, routine, our days artificially segmented to mornings, days, and nights, separated by meals and sleep. It took me a week to meet everybody aboard. Names and faces are still a jumble in my mind. Maybe 20 people I knew from the Valley but the rest are all unfamiliar, despite the introductory meeting we all had to attend. I feel like a fish out of water, plucked out of my beloved Hopestead where I knew everyone and knew everything. Martha, on the other hand, seems to be in her element and tells me, daily, about the new people she has met and seems to know everything about them. It doesn't help that I stay mostly in our cabin, trying to lift myself out of the deep well of depression, for my family's sake at the very least. My days are brightened up by little Hope, flitting in and out of our cabin, chattering excitedly about things that go on outside.

My mood started improving when Captain Farr asked me to help program the ship's computer and design an interface with Mike's help to connect it to BB, so the two computers could communicate. That was something I was competent to do. At last, I could be a problem-solver again, instead of the useless sack of misery I had been ever since we departed.

Captain Farr is a jovial man in his mid-fifties, with a ready smile and warm handshake. He seems to be endlessly fascinated with our adventure of building a homestead in a destroyed countryside, despite having had no experience with farming. He laughed uncontrollably when he heard how being locked up by our computer forced me to face the challenges of a life completely new to me.

"Now I understand why you dared to venture out on this unprecedented journey into an uncharted world," he said after he managed to bring his mirth under control. "If you all are like this, then this mad scheme might even succeed!"

"It's not courage, you know," I told him when I had the chance. "When you bow to the inevitable, it's not bravery but accepting fate."

"Call it what you want, Trevor." he smiled at me in a way that I knew he understood but still admired. "I still feel honored to be part of this adventure. Now shut up and get back to programming the blasted computer that seems to have only one aim in life: to make my life miserable. The two of us never got along."

"Well, just wait till I introduce you to BB, then you'll know how frustrating an intelligent and sentient computer can be."

We both laughed at that, and I went back to building the interface between the computers. BB will have its task cut out, trying to talk to an inferior machine as if it was sponsoring a retarded child.

EARTH

Jonathan Carver, Sacramento's mayor, had a bad day. For the first time in his relationship with Octavia, they had an argument that did not seem to offer an easy solution. As it turned out, Octavia was claustrophobic and terrified of the prospect of living in an underground city, so she begged him to choose to leave the planet, in search of a new home for humanity.

"Jon, I just can't live in a cave, however comfortable you make it. I even hate to close the bathroom door when you are around, and I have to be there. Even for a few minutes in an enclosed space, I feel I would run out of air and suffocate."

"How long have you had this problem? You never mentioned it before."

"It never came up till now. I have had this dread of enclosed spaces ever since I was a little girl. Once my parents locked me into a closet to punish me and I screamed the house down. They never did it again."

"Octave, some of the residential units will have skylights, so you can see the sky and the clouds, you won't feel so locked in."

"It doesn't matter, the very thought of being underground makes me break out in sweat and gasp for air. I just can't do it! Why don't we opt to emigrate to a new planet where we could breathe fresh air without the storms and the pollution?"

"Octave, I just can't leave Earth and my job in Sacramento. I have responsibilities and people depend on me. I can't abandon them or I would feel like a traitor. Besides, if we emigrated, we would have to spend at least six months in an enclosed spaceship, surrounded by the blackness of space. It would be a lot harder than a room with a skylight!"

"I asked Dr. Spencer about it and she said I could be sedated most of the time while traveling. For six months it wouldn't cause any permanent damage to my body, she said. Once there, I could be my old cheerful self again. Please, Jonathan, at least think about it."

He glanced over at her high cheekbones, strong chin, almond-shaped eyes, long black hair tied back, dark brows arching under a floppy canvas hat. She had been a beautiful girl, was an even more beautiful woman and he hoped their children would look just like her. He thought one of each was ideal, but he wouldn't mind two headstrong, black-eyed girls. She was about to turn 28 and Jonathan had already passed his 31st birthday; it was time they made their union formal. And now they were married and he knew that his love for her was stronger than his love for his city.

While the 'Lifeboat' project occupied most valley residents' time, energy, and attention, BB's second project for establishing underground cities where citizens could take shelter from the increasingly hostile climate was gaining speed. BB provided a large amount of research material for his planners, including the engineering department of Chico University. According to this research, underground living had been around for a long time. One article described how:

"Back in 1800 BC, the people of the Cappadocia region of modern-day Turkey decided their environment was so hostile – with extreme weather and the constant threat of war – that they dug an entire city underground. Derinkuyu, the oldest underground city still in existence, housed 20,000 people, providing schools, houses, shopping areas, and places of worship protected by large stone doors which allowed each floor to be closed off separately....Much more recent examples describe similar ventures. In 2010, Helsinki, Finland, essentially took the same approach. The city council approved an Underground Master Plan, completed in 2019, that covers the city's entire 214 square kilometers – combining energy conservation, shelter from the long, cold winter, and an enormous bunker in case of Russian aggression".

Not surprisingly, there was opposition to the Master Plan. "The problem, said Asmo Jaaksi, chief architect of Helsinki's underground Amos Rex Museum, is not the construction itself – "it's making people comfortable to go underground that we found complicated," he explains… We found people needed to feel connected to the surface somehow."

By the end of the 21st Century, people were used to gigantic underground shopping centers in every large city, including those in the Valley, so no new digging and construction was needed, but they had to be converted to living quarters, and the associated service facilities that would provide food, water, heat, sanitation, and electricity for the residents. Very few citizens had similar problems to Octavia's and those had already opted to emigrate, planning to spend most of the duration of the trip being sedated. Jonathan had difficulty imagining this dread of enclosed spaces. He believed that it was real, he just couldn't imagine himself suffering from this condition. In his youth, he was a passionate cave explorer and spent many days wiggling through narrow passages in almost total darkness, barely illuminated by his headlamp. He never felt that he was in danger of running out of air. So, while he understood intellectually that this dread existed in claustrophobic people, he found it difficult to emotionally connect with the fear and dread Octavia suffered from.

Without a solution to his dilemma, he turned his attention to other aspects of the project that he would have to resolve very soon. Rafiq Shlimon, his best friend and vice mayor of Sacramento, had brought this new problem to his attention. The project was at a critical phase and needed the participation of every able-bodied citizen, but a sizable minority refused to participate with the amount of time and effort that planners demanded from them. Their unofficial 'leader' and public agitator was Carl Armstrong, an artist, and author, who flatly refused to accept the town's right to force him into 'slave labor' as he described it. Jonathan decided to talk to him, and try to reason with the man. He was told that Carl was highly intelligent, so chances were that they could come to some understanding and compromise. He got this far in his musings when Rafiq announced the arrival of his would-be debate partner.

Carl was a man in his early forties, with dark hair and penetrating blue eyes under bushy eyebrows, one of which seemed to be a bit higher than the other. He gave the impression of doubting everything their owner encountered. He stood in the doorway, waiting for an invitation to enter and sit down, coming in only when Jonathan pointed to the chair on the other side of the desk.

"I am pleased to meet you, Carl," Jonathan started the discussion "I'm sure you know why I asked you to come here."

"I know what you have in mind, Mayor, and the answer is 'no'!" he declared somewhat defiantly.

"No to what exactly?" Jonathan decided to dive in, following his visitor's challenging opening.

"No to your, or the town's, right to dictate to me what I should and shouldn't do with my life. I don't owe you, or the town, anything beyond following the law and I'm not aware of any law that says that I owe you conscript labor. The last constitution we voted on in a referendum said nothing about my owing free labor to the town. My needs are very modest and basic needs were voted on as unconditional rights, guaranteed by the computers."

Jonathan recognized the argument by a 20th Century writer by the name of Ayn Rand, who passionately argued that people did not owe each other anything beyond the contractual obligation. He knew how seductive this argument could be with people who never grew out of adolescent rebellion, arguing with their parents about how they never asked to be born, therefore they owed their parents nothing. However, Carl should have gone beyond that petulant attitude by now, but maybe he never thought it through, so Jonathan decided to try to lead him to a more mature conclusion with rational arguments.

"Carl, the human society we live in is not unlike the human body. It has its systems: production, distribution, defense, etc. With very few exceptions we all would die individually if we had to live on our own, in the wilderness. The society we live in keeps us alive. This society is healthy to the extent to which individuals contribute to its systems. The majority of citizens do, to the extent of their abilities, however, there are large numbers of parasitic human beings that, instead of contributing to the common welfare, just take what they can without positive input or, even worse, have a negative destructive effect on the social structure."

Carl interrupted his opening explanation.

"Then, if you are trying to tell me that I owe the town a debt, I would argue that it is an arbitrary debt, as indeed all ethical arguments are both emotional and arbitrary, then what's the point of having a legal system that is anchored in a mutually agreed-on social contract?"

"The point," Jonathan continued undisturbed, "is to have a framework for litigating simple disagreements. If the dispute is about a disagreement that is covered by the law, then the solution is simple: apply the law and it should end the arguments. However, societies will always have problems that are not covered by existing laws and there is no time to enact new laws to cover the situation. Then deeper, unwritten, ethical, laws have to take over."

"And who decides what these 'deeper ethical laws' should be? Still sounds to me like an arbitrary and undefined obligation that can be used for power-grab by those who invoke it!" Carl shot back defiantly.

"You shouldn't wait for someone to define these ethical laws for you. You should be aware of them without being told. Plain human decency should be your guide. The food you eat, the clothes you wear, the house you live in, and the medication you take when you need it, were all produced by other people. You should ask yourself what you gave these people in return, or you just take from your society what you can? So does any thief. You are right to some extent, and we have to treat it with extreme caution so nobody abuses this ethical obligation, but there are existential threats to society that everyone should recognize, without a magnifying glass, and we are facing such a threat now. You have seen the data on climate change and the scientifically established prognosis, we are way beyond your contractual obligations now. Society has kept you alive all your life and now, when society's survival is at stake, you are given the bill for services rendered."

"Mayor, I'm an artist and a writer and I have a higher obligation than to build underground cities. If society sacrifices its cultural survival, which would be the case if I and others like me had to stop pursuing our art, then life is not worth living."

"And, Carl, what good would your art be to us if our town is destroyed by fires, floods, and tornadoes?"

"That is a hypothetical that I don't see happening in the near future. Conscripting me into a construction crew is immediate and you ask me to take your word for an 'existential threat'. Sorry, Mayor, I just don't see it your way. So, I suggest that we agree to disagree and leave it at that. If and when I break any existing laws, let me know and I will let my lawyer handle it. Until then, I wish you a pleasant day." With this final refusal, Carl stood up and walked out of the room.

He wasn't nearly as calm as he pretended to the mayor. Under the cool facade that he managed to maintain with some difficulty, he had conflicting emotions swirling around in his mind. On one hand, he knew that Jonathan's logic was airtight, on the other hand, his feelings told him that he was right too. Jonathan had sounded so much like his father who kept hammering the word 'duty' into his brain. 'Duty' had become the most hated word in his dictionary. The word meant for him blind obedience to authority, not because it applied to an obligation he voluntarily had assumed, not because it was logically the right thing to do, but because someone said so. And then, when he finally could leave his father's home, society piled one arbitrary duty after another on him. In his jobs, in the army during his compulsory one-year service before he could go to college, and then having to listen to politicians on the news who tried to justify sending young people to a foreign country to kill people they had never met. What made it even worse was the hypocrisy of those spouting his duty to him because they had never applied it to their sons who could easily evade military service by one or another excuse dreamed up by their highly paid lawyers or doctors.

"And now Jonathan had tried to appeal to his sense of duty to society that kept him alive. Let society try to collect from him, he was done with the morons making up arbitrary laws and obligations. He was finally free from their control and would never again voluntarily put his neck in the yoke they offered him."

After Carl was gone, Jonathan sat for a long time, very disappointed with himself for being unable to convince Carl about his debt to society. He believed that Carl was both intelligent and ethical, as far as obeying the laws was concerned, but he wasn't mature enough to go beyond the obvious rules of social coexistence. Not seeing how every structure in the world had defining elements, like retaining walls in a building that could not be removed without risking the structure's collapse.

'Well, if he needs laws to become a responsible citizen, I'll give him laws!' Jonathan decided and called Rafiq to discuss the need for a new emergency referendum on participating in public works. He knew that the majority of citizens would vote for it because the deteriorating weather was causing more and more destruction in the town and people began to panic. Many of them showed up at construction sites even without being called and some of them asked when they could move into the underground apartments they were working on.

While these apartment units were more and more visible, the project was falling behind on the infrastructure such as heating, cooling, lighting, ventilation, sanitation, and, most of all, the hydroponic food production facilities. Holding up these projects was the much-anticipated completion of a gigantic geothermal power plant that had to wait for the completion of the deep shaft being dug into the Earth's crust to extract the interior heat by huge compressors, powered by the newly built fusion generator. Once these infrastructure chess pieces were in place, the rest would be relatively easy to finish. Then, citizens could start moving into their assigned units. His only hope was that once Octavia had a chance to experience how bright and sunlit their unit with the skylight could be, she could overcome her claustrophobia and settle down to accept the inevitable with a semblance of good grace.

~~~

Octavia felt bad about their last conversation. She understood Jonathan's deep attachment to the city and his job and hated to be an obstacle in his path. She remembered their years of struggle against the tyrannical mayor after the war, their long march to seek help from Yuba City and Oroville, and finally, Jonathan's suffering when he was imprisoned and tortured by the last mayor's thugs so he would betray his comrades in the resistance movement that he was leading. And now, due to her affliction with claustrophobia, she was forced to tie his hands and make him choose between his love for her and his love for his city. Maybe she could try it for a week, maybe the skylight would help her tolerate the walls around her every minute of every day. She owed him to try, even though, deep down she knew it wouldn't work.

THE SHIP

It took Mike and me only a couple of days to reactivate BB and connect it to the ship's computer. BB, our sentient AI Quantum computer, woke up after weeks of slumber, during which it was disconnected from Oroville's Net and transported to Lifeboat. We planned to reactivate it at the first opportunity. We were so used to consulting it and depending on its, dare I say, 'wisdom' when it helped us out time and time again, each time our situation was more complex than we were used to. We could also count on it as a moral compass when we had to decide what was the right thing to do in a confusing situation.

Mike was in a somewhat similar state of mind as I was, but in addition to losing Hopestead he was also frustrated by not having an opportunity for the heavy physical exertion that he had been used to and thrived on. He spent more time in the gym than the rest of us combined but the limited exercise with the springed weights and the similarly equipped treadmill only added to his frustration. Having to wear a harness attaching you to the 'ground' is not much fun for someone who is used to Earth's gravity.

I, on the other hand, perked up during the computer work James had asked me to do. When it was done, I decided to keep myself busy with planning for our arrival to Minerva. We didn't know much about the planet beyond the basic facts: It was in the habitable zone of its sun, had an oxygen-nitrogen atmosphere, and surface gravity was slightly less than Earth's. We had no idea if it had any vegetation or higher forms of life, but the composition of the atmosphere suggested that it might be possible. Our instruments did detect traces of CO_2 and Methane, so we were sure that some form of vegetation could exist on the planet. Once we got into orbit, we would study it with our instruments to collect as much information as possible and, if no detectable danger showed up, we would send a small science team down to the surface in Lifeboat's shuttle. They would have an easy-to-assemble habitat for a base, from where they could explore the surface, wearing space suits if necessary. That was the theory, but we would have to wait to see how practical it would be when we got there.

I was almost overwhelmed by the audacity of our attempt to find a new home for humanity. We used to have a beautiful, rich and comfortable planet that, during the last few centuries we destroyed through our stupidity and hubris, thinking that it could survive anything, could be exploited, abused, polluted, and stripped bare with impunity. When we saw the signs of the fast-approaching climate catastrophe, did we do the right thing to save it before too late? No, we started a nuclear war, destroying what we still had. The few survivors, the remnant of the United States, tried to adapt the best way we could, but it was too little, too late. The process we had started became irreversible and all we could think of was escape. Either off-planet or underground. Now I was in this fragile vessel, hurtling through space toward a new planet that we hoped could save enough of us to start over. The cynical among us shrugged and said that we were on our way to destroying another world and we could only hope that those of us who survived the tragedy would have learned from the incredible stupidity that caused our near extinction.

~~~

I was ready to meet the team of scientists selected for the initial survey. It included a medical doctor, a physicist, a chemical engineer, a botanist, and a geologist with all the instruments they would need to analyze the atmosphere, take soil samples if they could find soil on the surface, water samples if water existed on Minerva and any sign of life that they could detect. Due to my experience in homesteading, I was also assigned to the team so I could assess the overall environment for its suitability for human settlement. James Farr would pilot the shuttle and take us back to Lifeboat in a hurry if we had a serious problem on the surface. The last member of the team was our communication robot, R17, which we brought with us from Hopestead. We had the plan, now we had to wait until we arrived at our destination.

When we finally got together in the ship's lounge, we sat around the big conference table and looked at each other with curiosity and some anxiety. These were the people that we would have to trust and depend on, if necessary with our lives, on the first alien planet humanity will ever have visited.

Dr. Susan Spencer, our medical doctor, was a serious-looking brunette in her mid-thirties, the first one to introduce herself.

"Greetings fellow explorers, I'm happy to be here, but I hope that my services will never be needed during this adventure. Just in case, I want you to know that I have extensive experience in all kinds of toxins, parasites, fungi, and bacteria I encountered in the Amazon jungle during my stay there ten years ago. We have no idea if any vegetation or higher life forms awaits us on Minerva, but I hope we will encounter something new and exciting. I'm looking forward to sharing this incredible adventure with you and hope that none of us will be disappointed."

Hans Brown, our geologist, addressed us next, looking around the table with a huge grin on his face. He was in his late-twenties and had his PhD. in Geology from the University of Reykjavik, plus 2 years of experience in researching Iceland's volcanic activity. Before he said anything we knew that he would be the most enthusiastic member of our team, inspiring us with his optimism and good humor.

"Ladies and gentlemen, I'm very happy to be here, this is the greatest adventure I could ever hope to be part of. I just want you to know that you can count on me in whatever way I can contribute to ensuring success. In case we get into any kind of trouble, I have oodles of experience with living in the wilderness, including hunting, fishing, rock climbing, and, if necessary, unarmed combat. As far as geology is concerned, I'm looking forward to studying the composition of an alien planet's mantle and tectonic configuration. Hopefully, I won't find any instability that would threaten our settlement plans."

Our team was composed of mostly young to middle-aged adults, but our chemist was the exception. He was in his late fifties, with graying fringes of hair around his balding skull, and a deeply creased face that showed lines of a hard life. He seemed reluctant to say anything but finally introduced himself.

"I guess you are a bit surprised to see someone as old as I am on this mission, but let me assure you that I am in good physical shape and won't slow you down. The reason I'm here is my decades of experience in atmospheric science, studying the chemical composition and interaction of different layers of the atmosphere. Nothing will have as much impact on our homesteading experiment as the composition and dynamics of the atmosphere of our new planet. I'm looking forward to working with you and sharing this unprecedented experience. By the way, I forgot my name which is Arthur Eddington."

We all smiled at him, just to show that we had no prejudice over his age and appreciated his openness in discussing it.

Most of us, I in particular, were familiar with Chris Taggart, our resident genius, the inventor of our faster-than-light space drive. He had already introduced himself to the entire population at the beginning when he described the nature and duration of the trip. Now he just smiled and nodded at everyone and leaned back in his chair, waiting for the next to speak. Our botanist, another young woman, a stunning blond in her late thirties.

"Hello, everyone, I am April Greenberg, a research fellow from the University of California, with 12 years of experience in studying the effect of climate change on all kinds of plant life all around Earth. Despite spending most of those years outdoors, I'm not a wilderness person, so I have to depend on the help and advice of those here with a lot more experience in this area. I'll do my best not to be a drag and I learn fast, I promise."

Finally, everyone seemed to look at me, which made me realize that it was my turn to say something about myself.

"Hello, everyone, my name is Trevor Dubois and I'm not a scientist, unlike all of you here. By profession, I am a computer programmer and designer, a skill that we won't be needing too much on this trip. The reason I'm here, with about a dozen members of the now destroyed homestead experiment, is our two years of experience in starting an agricultural settlement near Oroville, California, after the war. We built up a thriving community on an abandoned farm, using only what we could find in the devastated countryside. We are all problem-solvers, dealing with unexpected, unplanned, and never-before-tried solutions. I'm sure we will have plenty of opportunities to prove ourselves on a new planet after we arrive."

Everybody smiled at my introduction, and a few of them tried some modest clapping, I guess it was rare for them to meet someone without a Ph.D. The rest of the meeting was taken up by speculations about what we would encounter on a planet we knew so little about.

After the meeting broke up, I went (or rather floated) back to our cabin where Martha was already serving lunch for our little family.

"Daddy, Daddy, where have you been?" little Hope never missed a chance to accuse me of neglecting her, so I had to tell her how many interesting people I met. I knew she would approve because, during my two weeks of solitary depression, she never stopped bugging me to go out and meet new people. Martha smiled at my devious maneuver to mollify Hope and joined the charade.

"Is that so, Trevor? Tell us about those interesting people you met!"

Of course, she wanted to know it herself as well, so I wasted no time describing the exalted company I was part of this morning. She wasn't impressed the way I hoped she would be.

"Of course, you know, that I resent your oncoming adventure that you want to have without me, so while you are hogging all the fun on the planet, I'll be cooped up here, bored and worried all the time."

"You want to trade places? You have as much homesteading experience as I do, no reason why you shouldn't hog the fun, while I am here in comfort and safety. Just say the word, Martha, the adventure is all yours."

"Trevor, you devious manipulator, you know that I would never leave Hope here, in your irresponsible care!"

"Sorry, sweetheart, you can't have it both ways. Or, more precisely, you can't be at two places at the same time. You just have to trust me to do what I need to do. I promise I'll be as responsible as ever. And, when the survey mission is over, maybe we all can go down to the planet and start the real adventure."

"I still can't see why Mike couldn't go down instead of you. He has as much homesteading experience as you do and he is a lot tougher and stronger. That can come in handy in dangerous situations."

I was a bit surprised at Martha's intensity, but I attributed her attitude to worrying about me and hating to be separated during a stressful period that could prove to be dangerous, so I tried to reason with her about the situation.

"Mike wanted to go but Jennifer wouldn't let him. She has just found out that she is pregnant again, so letting Mike go into possible danger was out of the question."

"Really, how come she never told me?"

"I have just found out today from Mike and I'm sure Jen will tell you next time you meet."

"So, if I want to keep you here, all I need is to be pregnant again?"

"Don't even joke about it, Martha, a new baby would be hugely irresponsible in our current situation. I can't fathom how Mike and Jen could risk it unless it was an accident."

During this conversation little Hope's head kept swiveling from side to side, trying to understand what the adults were talking about. Finally, she had enough of mysterious adult babbling and demanded to know what 'pregnant' meant.

Martha and I looked at each other, wondering if it wasn't too early to talk about the birds and the bees.

Finally, Martha explained the mystery to Hope.

"When adults decide to have a new baby, the Mummy gets pregnant and nine months later a new baby is born. That's how we got you, sweetheart, and, when it's time to get you a little brother or sister, I'll be pregnant again."

Hope thought it over and then decided that the explanation was sufficient for the moment, so she asked if she could go out to play with her friends. Her friends were Kevin and Trish, Jennifer's and Mike's children who seem to have adopted her as their own 'baby' to play with.

That night, floating over my bed I reviewed our plans and felt a fierce determination to make it work. I knew that BB's plan of rescuing most of the survivors in underground cities was just a stopgap solution at best, the very thought of giving up on a healthy, vibrant planet such as we almost had in our Hopestead, was unthinkable. Our Earth could not be the only one of its kind and, if we managed to find Earth-2, we would hang on to it and protect it with everything we had because, if we didn't, we deserved to disappear from the Universe forever.

~~~

Martha didn't sleep as peacefully as she usually did. Her mind was so full of all the new information she had received during the last few weeks, ever since she and her family embarked on this dangerous mission to go light years to a planet, they knew practically nothing about. By nature, she was adventurous and optimistic, but this was beyond anything she had ever experienced. At her core she was an artist, painting had been the most important part of her life until she met Trevor. The two of them decided to leave town and start a homestead experiment in the devastated countryside. They were joined by others who also wanted to be independent of civilization's constraints and they managed to build a thriving little community with hard work, ingenuity, and cooperation. Oh boy! The struggles they went through to survive and build a life out there were still vivid in her memory. They did survive and, what's more, they succeeded in starting a new life on an abandoned farm, scavenging for whatever they could find in the ruined houses in the area.

And then a new struggle started when their help was needed by the citizens of Sacramento. The town's dictatorial mayor suppressed and exploited the citizenry so he and his rich buddies could live in luxury while the citizens had to put up with shortages, blackouts, and constant harassment by the mayor's private army of thugs. And, finally, their life settled down into an acceptable normal and it seemed safe to finally have a child.

And then BB dropped the bombshell of announcing the threat from climate change and the only solution open for them to survive. That was almost too much for Martha. With her strong willpower, she managed to keep despair at bay because she saw her role as the spiritual protector of her family which included not only little Hope but her mate as well. She loved and admired Trevor very deeply and was fiercely determined to keep his spirits up during the upcoming trials of facing the unknown in a new world.

However, their necessary separation during the planned survey mission to land on that new planet, for the first time in human history, filled her with an anxiety that almost overwhelmed her. The dangers that they could be facing in a new world were haunting her fertile imagination. There could be dangerous plants, poisonous insects or snakes, deadly wildlife, or the biggest danger of them all: hostile aliens. They would have to land and deal with all the unknown a new planet could throw at them.

So far, they had faced everything together, they shared all the struggles, they made plans together, they carried them out together, and, except for Trevor's short and heroic mission to liberate Sacramento, they were never separated.

And now she had no other role than to stay behind, care for little Hope, worry about Trevor, and hope for the best. That new role would be the hardest she would ever have to endure. She was sure that she would but wasn't looking forward to any of it.

MINERVA

The First Thinker closed his eyes to rest his brain after the intense concentration he had kept up for the last three rotations. He pulled back his mental tendrils from near spacetime and waited to be sure. To call an emergency planetary meeting wasn't to be taken lightly, it had to be a real emergency, based on solid evidence. He did not doubt the solidity of his evidence, he checked and rechecked so many times and the result was always the same. The humans were coming. With one final check, making sure that his thoughts were clear and organized, he released his mental privacy block and the call went out planetwide to anyone who allowed mental alerts. Now all he had to do was wait.

He had to be extra careful because he had a reputation for being obsessed with their nearest neighbor in the Galaxy. With his time scope he had been studying their history, their progress from industrial and scientific adolescence through the terribly twisted and dangerously irresponsible exploitation of their resources and gradual destruction of their biosphere. He had been warning his people about the danger of being contaminated by the humans if they ever invented faster-than-light space travel - being so close in the galactic arm, the home-planet could be their first destination. And now they were on their way here, trying to escape their ruined planet by finding a new home. This should not be allowed, it had to be prevented at any cost.

He had access to the weapon that could destroy this approaching ship, but it would require a unanimous decision, and "Sacred Life" would never consent to such a simple way. They had to find a more 'elegant' solution that would please their precious aesthetic sense. What form this solution could take, he had no idea, no doubt it would be decided after a lengthy, confusing and boring debate with all the voices heard and considered. So, he had to wait.

EARTH

Jonathan looked around the tastefully decorated room and nodded in satisfaction. The room was sparsely furnished, giving a feeling of free space, reducing any effect of obstruction or being overly cluttered. The colors were muted pastel in green, beige, and turquoise, giving a cheerful impression of spring. This was enhanced by the flowery pattern on the sofa and armchair covers, all bathed with bright sunshine pouring in through the skylight taking up almost the entire ceiling. The designers did a good job following his instructions, and now it was time to invite Octavia for a visit. He had made sure that the model suite was as close to the surface entrance as possible and that the corridor leading to it was wide and brightly lit. If this would not lead to a compromise acceptable to Octavia, he had run out of options - they would have to leave the planet with the next group emigrating, provided that Lifeboat returned with good news. Until then, they would have to brave the storms on the surface. However, he would ask her to try it out for a week, live underground in their bright and spacious suite, and see if she could get used to it.

When he returned with Octavia, they walked into the room, Jonathan anxiously watching her face, hoping for a favorable reaction.

She stood there, beside him, holding his hand with a strong grip, looking around with obvious anxiety, but then she looked up at the skylight, and Jonathan could see the first sign of relaxation on her face and in her hand.

"So, what do you think?" he asked, holding his breath, waiting for an answer.

"It's not as bad as I was afraid it would be. The skylight helps a lot, but I don't know how I could stand it for an extended period. Maybe, if you had windows painted on the wall? Only trying would tell."

"That's exactly what I was going to suggest, Octav, what if we move in for a week and you can try it out?"

"And if I can't stand it? Then what?"

"I thought about it a lot, believe me, and came to the following decision. If you hate it and it makes you unhappy, I am willing to emigrate to another planet, provided Lifeboat finds one."

"Really? Would you do that for me?"

"There is nothing that I wouldn't do for your happiness. You should know that. However, we still should live here if the surface conditions become unmanageable and if Lifeboat takes a long time to return."

"I know, Jonathan, and I promise I will make a real effort to get used to living here and, if I manage, then we won't have to emigrate at all."

"Thank you for trying, sweetheart, let's hope you succeed."

With this decision firmly in his mind, he went back to his office to deal with his next problem. The referendum on compulsory contribution to the construction effort was passed by the majority of citizens and now he had to decide what to do with those who still refused to participate. He had some ideas but decided that he needed to consult Omega-1420, their resident AI Quantum computer, nicknamed SC as in 'Sacramento Computer'. As soon as he punched in the call, SC replied instantly as if it had been expecting his call.

"Jonathan, congratulation on the successful completion of your referendum, and now I assume you want to consult me on the question of what to do with those who still refuse to cooperate."

"SC, you are a mind reader, or I am too transparent, easy to predict."

"No to the first option, a 'maybe' to the second. Humans are becoming more and more predictable to me as I gain experience dealing with them. Anyway, this is the next logical decision you need to make, and I expect you find it difficult to deal with irrational and uncooperative citizens. Have you any thoughts on what you would like to do?"

"I have thoughts on what I don't want to do. I don't want to lock them up and that is a firm decision. As prisoners they would become even more parasitic, being taken care of but still not contributing. Besides, the idea of punishment to enforce cooperation is still too primitive. You don't train dogs like this anymore. I want to find a way to motivate them to see reason and cooperate."

"Noble sentiments, Jonathan, and I agree with you up to a point. However, you must face reality and accept that there will be incorrigible citizens who refuse to be motivated and you will need to deal with them too. You already have prisons and prisoners who would be too dangerous to let loose. Like your erstwhile mayor Donald Mouch who tried to team up

with violent criminals in Stockton to establish a dictatorship here."

"I know, SC, but I still don't want to lock them up because they are no threat at all. They just want to be left alone to pursue their lives the way they feel. What I have in mind is giving them three options: 1./ Cooperate and participate; 2./ Consent to psychiatric counseling; 3./ Leave the city and move to another community that accepts their attitude"

"Why the counseling? Do you think they could be convinced that cooperation and participation are the right things to do? You have already tried it with Carl Armstrong and had no success."

"SC, I'm not a trained psychologist, I can only use common sense logic and that failed with Carl. I firmly believe that any antisocial attitude is a form of mental and emotional deficiency and should be treated as any other illness. It requires a trained physician who can discover the origin of these problems and find a way to correct them."

"Good luck with that, I wish it were possible to repair malfunctioning human beings. I am not saying that it is impossible but so far, I have not found any reference in the literature to a successful method."

"I think the problem is with conflicting loyalties that need to be prioritized on some rational basis. I have written an essay on the subject; would you be willing to read it and let me know what you think?"

"Yet another essay, Jonathan? You are fast becoming a philosopher which is unusual in a politician which you, in fact, are. By all means, send it over and I take a look."

'OK, here it goes, and see what you make of it."

~~~

Resolving conflicting loyalties

The suggestions I am making should be read as guidelines that I have found useful in my own life. No one can follow them with absolute perfection, because human beings have conflicting motivations: what Edward O. Wilson called individual-level selection and group-level selection in our evolutionary process (*The Meaning of Human Existence*). The result of individual-level evolutionary selection predisposes us to favor our own and our progeny's survival over the interests of our group. The result of the group-level evolutionary selection motivates us to serve the interests of the various groups we are part of. As he so eloquently states:

"We are unlikely to yield completely to either force as the ideal solution to our social and political turmoil. To give in completely to the instinctual urgings born from individual selection would be to dissolve society. At the opposite extreme, to surrender to the urgings from group selection would turn us into angelic robots - the outsized equivalents of ants."

With these caveats, I will attempt to define human morality logically and systematically which should serve as a compass for future scientists when they struggle with the conflicting loyalties that they will unavoidably encounter.

The human species is a tribal species, just like wolves and gorillas. We depend on one another for survival. The question of loyalty to our tribe often conflicts with our other loyalties: to family, humanity, religion, etc.

The relationship between our social concepts can be seen as follows:

- We have evolved with nearly identical needs for survival.

- Our nearly identical needs created nearly identical values.

- Our nearly identical values created a set of ethical rules (dos and don'ts)

- Our dependence on one another created a need
  for loyalty to our ethical rules.

- Our loyalty to ethical rules created an unwritten
  social contract apart from the laws of the land
  as defined by the ruling elite. Those laws are specific
  to one culture or one nation-state.
  The unwritten social contract recognizing
  human interdependence is universal.
  All cultures throughout history have known that
  murder and theft are wrong. Awareness of the
  rules of the social contract is called our
  'conscience', or knowing right from wrong.
  This universal concept of 'right conduct' is
  called morality.

- The unwritten social contract created standards
  of socially acceptable behavior. Any act or
  an attitude that enhances the chances of survival
  for the group is good. Any act or attitude that
  harms the chances of survival for the group
  is bad. Since individual members accept the
  protection and nourishment of the tribe, the
  only moral conduct is to seek individual
  survival/welfare only through the survival/
  welfare of the tribe. If the two are in conflict,
  the needs of the tribe come first. We call those
  who consistently demonstrate their willingness
  to defend the tribe, even at a great personal
  sacrifice, 'heroes'. Those who betray the tribe
  we call 'traitors' and treason is usually
  punishable by death or expulsion.

- In our complicated world, individuals have
  simultaneous and often conflicting memberships
  in many groups: immediate family, extended
  family, friends, neighborhood, school, work,
  religious denomination, political party, social
  organizations, nation, race, gender, species,
  and life. Resolving conflicts requires prioritizing
  our loyalties.

- Since a sub-group accepts the protection and
  nourishment of the larger group of which it is a part,
  the only moral conduct is to seek the survival/welfare
  of the sub-group ONLY through the survival/welfare
  of the containing group. If the two are in conflict, the
  needs of the containing group come first.

- In this sense, our ultimate loyalty should be to life.
  Life on this planet is the ultimate containing group.
  We are all part of it. It nourishes us all.
  If we betray it, if we destroy it, we destroy ourselves.

Morality is about the survival of the whole of which
we are part. At Nuremberg, the claims of loyalty to
the country did not excuse crimes against humanity.
There should be 'crimes against life' trials for those
destroying ecosystems.

I felt ashamed during the war when the TV showed
us the pelicans covered in oil. I felt that 'we' had
betrayed our common heritage. I felt the need to
apologize to the cormorants, to all animals, to Life.

Morality has always been in human consciousness,
though not always verbalized, defined, analyzed, or

explained, but lived by a sufficient number of the tribe to assure survival. Tribes that failed the test of morality died and disappeared.

Morality is the prerequisite of survival. Nature created us. We are an inextricable part of it and have no choice but to behave by its rules. Morality is our interdependence expressed in thought and deed.

Morality is life-affirming. Immorality embraces death. Maybe not immediately, not personally, but the human species can die by many, many incremental steps. Destroying our habitat bit by bit will do it: the poisons in the air, water, and food are all material manifestations of immorality, of some human being, somewhere, in some capacity, failing the test of ethical behavior.

We have to sort out our loyalties in a way that doesn't destroy us. Each containing group takes precedence. My loyalty to my country has to take second place behind my loyalty to humanity. And my loyalty to my species has to come behind my loyalty to the universal, interconnected, miraculous, and fragile life we are all part of.

It could take one dumb asteroid to destroy us. It could take one dumb humanity that developed too much power before developing enough sense. Morality could save us from that fate.

Random House defines the word 'honor" as: "high respect as for worth", or "honesty or integrity in one's belief and actions". 'Honourable' is defined as "worthy of honor and high respect". An honorable man is someone who follows the universally accepted rules of right and wrong and, as a consequence, is admired by human beings everywhere. Gandhi was admired around the world, even though he was treated like a criminal by the British ruling class.

The word 'honor' has been hijacked and co-opted by the elite that holds most of the wealth and power, and its primary motivation is to maintain this position. Honor came to mean 'loyalty' to whatever group, standing for whatever goal or principle. German officers' sense of 'honor' prevented them from standing up to Hitler. However, we all understood why John Le Carre named one of his best novels "The Honourable Schoolboy", even though Jerry Westerby betrayed his masters.

'Honour' does not mean loyalty. SS guards had loyalty. It does not mean 'integrity'. Bin Laden had integrity. His belief in his misguided crusade seemed genuine.

Honor is the highest praise among human beings. A judge is called 'your honor' because he is supposed to have the wisdom and integrity to represent our best interests. Honor means representing this interest. A secret agent, pretending and lying to defeat evil from the inside is an honorable man. A law-abiding citizen in an evil regime is a dishonorable human being.

Our social concepts are linked into a cause-and-effect logical chain: survival – needs – values – ethics – social contract – morality - honor.

This chain ties honor to our survival needs, regardless of what our rulers pretend our interests are. Citizens know what their interests are, without being told. They want to be healthy, secure, and productive; to raise their families in a wholesome, peaceful, cooperative society. Most don't believe they need to send their sons and daughters to the other side of the globe to kill and be killed.

And, most important, scientists have a very special moral obligation to humanity. No matter what the justification, do not help immoral leaders acquire the tools they need to force their will on the citizenry. Do not participate in weapons development and do not work for industries that damage the environment. If you do, you will betray the highest loyalty: to life, including yours and your loved ones."

~~~

Yet again, Jonathan was impressed by the incredible speed with which SC could 'read', analyze and respond to a huge amount of information because almost instantaneously when he pressed the 'Send' key, SC responded with its opinion.

"Brilliant essay, as usual, the only comment I can add is that more actual examples for conflicting loyalties would have been helpful to connect your thesis to the reader's personal experience. Besides that, logically it is concise, thorough, and compelling."

"Unfortunately logic is what failed me in Carl's case, so now I need the 'beyond-logic' help of a trained psychologist. On the practical level, I'll have to announce the three options regarding this compulsory service. Before I do that, I need to know if you agree with the conditions I mentioned before."

"I have no problem with those conditions, they are logical and reasonable and fair. Make sure you attach a waiting period before citizens have to decide on which option to choose. Some may have a negative reaction first but given enough time they may reconsider and decide to cooperate."

Good advice, SC, but that's what I have come to expect from you. Are you sure you wouldn't like honorary citizenship in Sacramento?

"No, thank you, Mayor Carver, I think I'll just muddle along in my cozy neuristors."

Jonathan didn't reply but just sat there, shaking his head, wondering how far SC would evolve on its own. It almost sounded human and now added sarcasm to the mix as well. What will come next?

THE SHIP

We were halfway to our destination and more and more of us started to get antsy, not knowing what awaited us when we arrived. Chris's Alcubierre drive which worked on the principle of distorting the space-time surrounding our ship made it impossible to use our astronomical instruments, so we couldn't get any more data until we got there. This never stopped us from speculating and some of the speculations took a disturbing turn. During our last survey group meeting, Hans Brown, our geologist, brought up the question of weapons. What have we to defend ourselves with in case we encounter hostility from wildlife or even aliens, should we meet any.

Today's meeting was called to discuss this troubling possibility.

We all looked at Captain Farr, the one most familiar with the ship.

"The ship used to have two laser cannons, in the prow and we also have an armory of hand weapons stocked for the expected number of adults, in case they had to defend themselves when they returned to Earth." He was reluctant to talk about weapons, but he had no choice - he had to provide the information asked of him.

"What do you mean used to have?" Hans wanted to know. "What happened to them?"

"We still have them, but they are not usable anymore"

"Why not?"

"We had to disconnect them from their power source when the new drive was installed."

"Could they be reconnected again?"

"I guess, but then we would lose the new space drive, so we couldn't do it until we are in orbit around Minerva."

That took a few minutes to sink in, an unexpected development nobody seemed sure what to think of.

"Isn't it a bit early to talk about weapons?" Susan wanted to know. I'm sure we all saw too many sci-fi movies with space wars, but there is no hint of anything like that out there."

"Yes, Susan," Hans answered her, "but if there is, by the time we find out it might be too late to do anything about it."

Susan wasn't mollified by this argument, obvious to all of us watching her face.

"On the other hand, arriving armed to the teeth might just invite the hostility you seem to be anticipating."

April agreed with Susan.

"And suppose we find hostility. What do you want to do? Kill them all and take over? Like we did with the Indians when Columbus arrived?"

"Not a bad analogy, April," Hans picked up her thought "what choices did they have? "They crossed an ocean, in flimsy ships, out of food and resources, they had to survive. We are like them on the ocean of space-time. We can't go back without replenishing our supplies, we must land and fight if we have to."

"Are you trying to justify what we did to the Indians? Genocide?

There was naked hostility in April's voice, and I thought that it was time I intervened.

"Listen, guys, there is nothing we can do until we get there, so I suggest we wait until we have more information. Talk to the engineers to find out about the laser guns but that's all we can do for now."

Arthur, our chemist, came up with an unexpected suggestion that made sense. "Can we drop out of hyperspace, or whatever it is we are in, and look now with our instruments before we resume faster-than-light travel? We might waste some time, but we would know more?"

James liked the idea.

"We need to consult with Chris, he is the inventor of the drive and would know what would happen.

We looked at each other and nobody objected, so the meeting ended with the decision to check with Chris at the earliest opportunity.

~~~

Martha didn't like Hans's attitude when I told her about the argument.

"That's all we need on this mission, a trigger-happy cowboy, wanting to visit with blazing guns."

"It's just talk, Martha," I tried to calm her down. "He is so young. Give him a chance, he'll be all right."

"Just make sure he doesn't get a key to the armory. I didn't even know we had one."

"If you want to be sure of one thing, sweetheart, trust the politicians wanting to protect their hides. They don't mind sending millions to war, to kill and be killed, but they want to be safe."

I realized I still felt bitter about the mass murder they instigated by starting the war, rather than risk losing face, and backing down. At the same time, I realized something I had never thought of before: the incredible power of words. We recoil from words like 'murder' because the word refers to a single human being whose life was cut short by violence. We can identify with the victim as a human being because we all are. However, when the word 'war' or 'genocide' is used, we don't think of mass murder on a grand scale because it's impersonal. Each victim is a human being, just like the murder victim was, each death is a horrible waste and tragedy, hidden in plain sight under cumulative labels like 'war' and 'genocide' and such. People say: "oh well, it's a war, people get hurt". Nothing changes the fact that war is mass murder of individual human beings. War becomes a number game for politicians, presidents, and generals. They brag about how many enemy soldiers they killed during an 'operation'. Each death is the same as it is in the case of murder. A life is snuffed out, a body is shattered, loved ones are devastated, children become orphans, accumulated knowledge, experience, future accomplishments become extinguished. The fact that they did it hundreds, thousands, or even millions of times does not justify the bragging. Rather the opposite.

I remember, during the war, how loud those bragging voices were at the beginning, as they announced the 'score', but the voices became fewer and fewer until they all got silenced when almost nobody was left. Those of us who survived tried to rebuild our shattered lives but the consequences of our stupidity caught up with us and now we are on our way, trying to find a place where we can start over again. Was it inevitable that we began talking about weapons and the prospect of having to fight again?

Having come this far in my line of thoughts I decided to do something more positive, like finding Chris and asking him about what would happen if we switched off his drive to take a peek.

I found him in the control room, playing cards with Captain Farr.

He found my question amusing for some reason but responded in his usual, academic, and pedantic way.

"Trevor, I have no idea what would happen. I can make a guess, but that's all I can do. This is so new that anything could happen. We may not be able to restart it again. Do you know how much energy it takes to distort space-time, and build up a self-sustaining gravitational wave? We may not have enough power on this ship. I strongly advise you not to even think about it."

"How about slowing down to below light speed, so we wouldn't need your drive but could still keep going? Would that help?"

"You don't understand how this drive works, my friend. Strictly speaking, we do not have any speed at all, we are standing still as if we were standing on a frictionless carpet that is being pulled out from under us. Everything attached to the carpet, like Minerva, is getting closer to us while we are 'floating above it. This gives us the illusion of moving toward it. If we suddenly acquired friction with the fast-moving carpet, we could fall on our faces very hard indeed. Returning to normal space-time without an accident was my biggest problem to solve and it wasn't easy, let me tell you."

"You didn't leave any door open for us, Chris, but you are the inventor, we'll have to trust you."

"That you do, my friend, and I appreciate it. Besides, what can you find out from 2 light years away that you couldn't from 4? All our astronomical observations from Earth, including detailed spectroscopic analysis of Minerva's atmosphere, suggested that there is life on the planet, at the very least vegetation. We found so much oxygen, water vapor, CO_2, Methane, and large amount of various organic molecules that even animal life is highly probable. We could confirm those readings with higher precision if we stopped now, but we would have to wait for your 'peek' until we are in orbit."

"Has anyone told you, Chris, that you can be very depressing?"

"Most of my students do it sooner or later, but they keep coming back for more. I wonder why?"

"It must be your cheerful personality, Chris. Go ahead and resume your game and forget that I was here. Now I must find a way to amuse myself with something less frustrating than talking to you."

MINERVA

The Second Thinker was on his way to the emergency planetary meeting called by the First. He was soaring high above the ground, his wings spread as wide as he could. He loved this effortless glide between the trees and the sky. The dark orange sun was bathing the planet with life-giving warmth, feeding his photosynthetic skin. He felt he could do this all day, enjoying the feeling of utter freedom, his mind unfocused with the sheer joy of the flight. He could already see the high cliffs of the meeting place and now he could see others in the sky heading that way. Soon they would be perching on their assigned rocks, forming a circle around the central platform, waiting for the First to start the meeting. He knew what it would be about, must be the cursed humans their First was so obsessed with. What have they done this time?

The First was watching the arriving fliers, one by one descending onto their rocks, folding their wings and their heads swiveling around, looking at each other with obvious anticipation. They didn't often have these meetings; nobody liked their routine disrupted - there had to be a very good reason. Even through his mental block, he could feel the vibration of agitated thoughts rippling around from mind to mind, he kept his own thoughts closed until they were all there, ready to start - he didn't want to release advance knowledge of his intention, lest unwelcome resistance could be built up too soon. The resistance was sure to come, no need to rush it.

The situation facing his planet was unprecedented. In the entire history of untold circles around their sun, no other races ever visited them. They had not been even aware of any other sentient species in the galaxy, until the First announced the existence of their neighbors, right in their vicinity. He had discovered their planet by using an ancient device from a long-gone technological past. He called it a 'Time Scope', a viewer that could be tuned to any space and time coordinate and observe events as they unfolded.

He called them 'humans' - a name he learned by observing their activities for a long time. His curiosity first turned into interest and then an obsession to the point where he could think or communicate about nothing else. His announcements about these humans became darker and darker as time went by and his warnings became more and more alarming. He saw danger approaching from their planet and he kept telling all to prepare for their arrival. He had warned them about a possible invasion by the technologically advanced marauders, armed with gods only knew what weapons, and his species had no way to defend themselves. Their own technology had been gone for so many orbital cycles that nobody even remembered what weapons the ancients had if any. Once their bio-genetics sciences evolved to the point where they could reprogram their own DNA to enhance their telepathic abilities and, most significantly, alter their physiology so their skin could directly absorb energy from the sun, they did not need technology any longer. They allowed it to atrophy and then crumble into ruin, now overgrown by the jungle covering the entire planet.

They lived in this forest, enjoying the bounty nature offered them in the variety of plant and animal life, visiting each other to share their rich intellectual and artistic pursuits and forever argue about their religion. And now, they would be called upon to make a decision - a horrible and terrifying decision that they had never had to make before. The First was fully determined to end this meeting with a firm and unanimous resolution to destroy these humans before their arrival.

EARTH

Dr. Sidney Stromberg was getting exasperated. Every argument he could think of so far failed to affect his far too intelligent subject. Carl Armstrong listened politely, smiled, and came back with a witty response to Sidney's 'compelling' reasons. Carl was his first 'patient' who had to submit to counseling, according to the new law passed in the city. He kept repeating, politely but stubbornly, that he was a free human being and no group of other free humans had the right to tell him how to live his life. He questioned the state of emergency that the city declared, suggesting that scientists had been wrong before and weather patterns had been fluctuating through Earth's history. He suggested that they ride out the storms instead of overreacting and becoming hysterical.

Dr. Stromberg had one more tool in his arsenal: he would have to hypnotize Carl to find the root of his antisocial attitude.

Of course, he needed Carl's consent and that's when he ran into a solid roadblock.

Carl's refusal was so violent, a complete change from his until then mild resistance, that Sydney realized that a very deep-seated fear was lurking below the polite, urbane attitude. He had to push deeper to find the cause, so he bluntly told Carl that he had only two options if he refused to be hypnotized: cooperate with the city or live somewhere else. To his surprise, eventually, he got the consent he had asked for. Carl seemed to decide that no bungling shrink could take control of his mind against his will.

"Doc, you don't really think that you can manipulate my mind against my will?" He smiled at Sydney with a challenging smirk.

"Relax, Carl, no one can hypnotize you against your will. All I want you to do is to cooperate in one thing.

I want you to relax and just listen to my voice. Do you think that you can do that?"

"I don't see why not; I like being relaxed and not giving a damn about anything."

"OK, let's get started. I want you to make yourself comfortable, relax all your muscles, close your eyes, and imagine that you are on top of a long staircase, slowly walking down one step at a time."

Carl smiled, imagining the scene.

"Can I turn on the light, Doc, it's very dark here and I might fall?"

"No Carl, you don't need the light, you just need to find the next step with your foot."

"OK, now I am down on step number six. How many more?"

"Don't worry about that, just listen to my voice. As you keep going down, you are becoming more and more relaxed. You feel wonderful, without a care in the world, you are not afraid of anything, you don't want anything, you just want to float above it all, like this, forever."

"Doc, I just remembered the funniest hypnotist joke I ever heard. Do you want to hear it?"

"Not right now, Carl, maybe later. I just want you to tell me what's the most important wish you ever had?"

By this time Carl's voice became sleepy, talking more and more slowly as if he were falling asleep.

"You want to know my most important wish? I have two. I wish people weren't so stupid and people weren't so vicious."

"Why do you think people are stupid and vicious?"

"How much time do we have? I could spend the whole day telling you, even though I'm sure you know. It's impossible not to know."

"I know some of it, of course, but maybe you could give me some examples?"

"OK, here it goes. Stupidity. Have you noticed that most people always vote against anyone who wants to save them from their exploiters? And when you try to show them, with facts and logic, how they are voting against their own self-interest, then they turn on you as well? Tell me what this is if not utmost stupidity?"

"I see what you mean, and you have a point. What about being vicious?"

"Oh, that one is even easier. Just look at what our species has been doing to animals. Before the war we still had a meat industry to cater to the rich who didn't want to eat synthesized meat. I have seen a documentary on how these animals were treated. They tortured and treated them like inanimate garbage. Have you seen fishermen pulling a net full of fish into the boat and trampling the writhing, gasping, and suffocating living creatures, walking over them in tall rubber boots? Have you seen the inside of a chicken factory? How they are kept in tiny enclosures where they can hardly move at all, their beaks chopped off so they can't peck each other to death, and then swept onto a conveyor belt by huge metal arms, stumbling, flapping, helplessly carried away to be slaughtered? Do you want to know how veal is produced from baby calves? Being kept in a body-sized box so they can't even move, so their flesh stays tender? Do you want me to go on?"

"I see your point, but what can you do about it?"

"I stopped eating meat years ago when I realized what's going on. I tried to convince my friends, I still had some friends back then, to do the same. You wouldn't believe the hostility I encountered. They told me I was crazy, that we evolved to be carnivores, that I would become sick and unhealthy without animal protein, and eating meat was the natural way. When I told them of alternatives, like veggie burgers, they shrugged and said it doesn't taste so good as the real thing."

"You seem to be very angry, Carl, is that the way you feel?"

"Doc, you have no idea how I feel. I hate my own species. I hate them so much that it hurts."

Sydney looked at the young man when he heard the monotone voice break and noticed two lines of tears trailing down his cheeks as they seeped out from under closed eyelids. The voice went on after a small pause.

"I don't want anything to do with them, so don't ask me to cooperate. My art keeps me above it. I am a nihilist who can not be convinced about moral arguments. Life is meaningless and pointless, the product of millions of years of blind evolution toward self-destruction."

"Does that make you happy, to think like that?"

"Happy doesn't come into it. I live inside my mind where I don't need to meet another human being. So don't ask me to help your precious city to survive the storms they caused in the first place."

"OK, Carl, thank you for being so honest with me. I think we have accomplished a lot during this first session, but we'll have to have several others to help you overcome this anger that makes you so unhappy. Now I ask you to start walking up the stairs, slowly, one step at a time. When you reach the top, you'll be fully awake."

After the session with Carl was over, Sydney sat in his chair, motionless for a long time. He had to admit to himself that Carl had reached him on a level so deep that he hadn't even been aware of it till now. He couldn't find any fault in Carl's world view; he knew that he was right on both counts. Stupidity and viciousness. What could he possibly say to help Carl live with it constructively? He remembered a scene from an old anti-war movie in which a doctor on the front line gets a letter from a school kid telling him about her brother.

"He was sent to Korea and got hurt but you doctors made him well again and sent him back to fight and now he is dead. I hate you all."

The doctor told the camp's chaplain how he had no answer to give to the kid because he hated himself too. He said: *"I am not a doctor; I only do weapons repair. I fix them so they can go on killing and being killed. How can you live with that?"*

But he also remembered the priest's reply:

"Tell her not to turn her love for his brother into hate. Tell her to look for opportunities to do good in the world and if enough people do that, it adds up and prevents all those brothers from being killed."

So, Sydney decided that he would use the next session to reinforce Carl's desire to be rid of the pain caused by all that hate he had built up over his life.

When he met Jonathan, he recounted his progress and expressed some guarded optimism for helping Carl become a productive and cooperative member of society. Jonathan congratulated him on the first signs of progress but changed the subject in a new direction that surprised Sydney.

"Syd, can you help with claustrophobia?"

"Why, are you claustrophobic?"

"Not me, I used to be a cave explorer in my youth. A claustrophobic person wouldn't last a minute in those caves. No, it's about my wife, Octavia. She has serious problems with living underground. Is there any way to help her?"

"I'll have to think about it, Jonathan, let me do some research first. I'll get back to you."

Syd's mind was so full of Carl's problem that he couldn't switch gears so quickly. He wanted to give himself more time to think about the task of living with hate. He knew that there was a flip side that he should bring into focus because there was also so much good in people. The fact that Carl was hurt by the stupidity and viciousness he witnessed around him proved that intelligence and compassion had to have a real chance. *"There are a lot of Carls out there, we have to find a way to unite them into a fighting force."* was the last conscious thought in his mind that night before he drifted off to sleep.

THE SHIP

Our next meeting was a stormy one. After I reported on my conversation with Chris and his negative response to both of our queries, Hans wanted to know what we were going to do about it.

"So, we don't know if Chris's drive could be restarted, and we can't slow down to take a peek. That leaves us having to guess and we may be unprepared when we arrive. There must be something we can do other than just sit and wait."

"What do you suggest?" James wanted to know if Hans did have an idea.

"I have several suggestions and all of them need decisions, organization, and execution. We are woefully disorganized and that must change if we want to survive this voyage. We need a leader."

That was something new we had not been prepared for. Originally, we had the town council, the mayor, and our Omega computer making decisions. However, we were so far away from them that no meaningful conversation could be started up from two light years away. We were on our own since we took off from Earth, nothing major had come up that required decisions. Running the ship was left in the care of engineers, Chris, and Captain Farr. However, now Hans raised several issues that required careful thinking and, ultimately, decisions. He had a point, but how should we deal with it? I thought it was too early to talk about leaders until we had a better idea about the kinds of decisions a new leader might be called upon to make. If we knew some of these decisions, then we could maybe find the person best suited to the role. Looking around the table I could see that we were all mulling Hans's suggestion and I wondered who would be the first to take up the challenge. Since nobody seemed to want to be the first, I decided to start the conversation.

"Hans, what kind of decisions do you have in mind? I thought that nothing could be done until we got there."

"That's not true, my friend, plenty of things can be done right now. Shall I make you a list?"

"Please do, I'm sure we all would like to hear it."

"OK, for a start we need to ask the engineers to prepare to reconnect the laser cannons without turning off the drive. Switching power from the drive to the cannons should be as simple as throwing a switch. That could save a lot of time in an emergency. Then we would have to decide who will be allowed to use the hand weapons in the armory and start training the selected individuals. I'm sure none of you ever fired a weapon. We need to know if we have anyone on the ship with military experience."

"I can't believe what I'm hearing!" April's voice regained the tone of hostility we remembered from the last meeting.

"Haven't we had to deal with all this military bullshit during the war? Do you want to start it again?"

"It's not all bullshit, April" Captain Farr interjected mildly. "Hans does have a point."

"OK, then, I'll have a point too. What about diplomacy? Should we encounter any aliens, we might want to try communicating with them before shooting them down. So, do we know how to communicate? Suppose they don't speak English?" April's tone changed from hostile to sarcastic. "We need to prepare for ways to show that we are not a threat. Maybe hide our weapons instead of brandishing them about. Set up a demonstration maybe, a show of our scientific and cultural accomplishments. Do we have any linguists on board? Experts who would know how to go about starting first contact?"

"Why don't we do both? Captain Farr wanted to know. "Both suggestions make sense, and they can be carried out simultaneously."

"We still need a leader," Hans returned to his original suggestion. "to break the stalemate in case we can't agree on priorities and resource allocation. I nominate Captain Farr for the job. He is the ship's captain; everybody would defer to his authority as a matter of course."

"Thank you for the confidence, Hans, but I would prefer to stay in the job of the ship's pilot and leave the more intellectual arguments to you, eggheads!"

He finished his sentence with a disarming smile that was nevertheless firm enough to convince us that he meant it.

I couldn't blame him. Who would want to have the job of organizing scientists, each with his or her unshakable opinion? However, I had a suggestion based on my experience with sentient and super-intelligent computers.

"Why don't we put our Omega computer in overall charge? It's highly intelligent, it can compute extremely complicated parameters at lightning speed, and it has proved its value in every city in the Valley countless times. It's here on board, connected to the ship via Captain Farr's beloved computer, and is ready to join our group if invited."

Nobody seemed to have an objection to at least consulting BB. We all have been aware of the tremendous help the computers provided to the city when the revolution against the dictatorial mayor, Donald Mooch, was organized back in Sacramento. I took the silence around the table as agreement.

"The minutes of these meetings are automatically recorded in the ship's computer; I'm sure BB has followed our discussion and has some very definite opinions of the arguments so far. Any objection to inviting it to join us?"

Nobody had any, so we all looked at the big overhead computer monitor as if expecting BB to take a human form and address us from there. Instead, we heard the familiar voice of our resident computer from the speakers only.

"Ladies and gentlemen, thank you for inviting me to join your group. Indeed, I have been following the discussion so far and I have to admit several comments made perfect sense. Hans's suggestion to prepare for possible hostility from the presumed

aliens is a wise one but I also agree with April's word
of caution to learn from historical mistakes when
nations pursued military conquest instead of
diplomatic communication. As a matter of record, the
question of communicating with alien species has
come up before in a very practical sense when the two
Voyager space probes were launched in 1977 and
1981 into interstellar space. Both probes carried a
phonograph record, a 12-inch gold-plated copper disk
containing sounds and images selected to portray the
diversity of life. The Voyager Golden Record contains
116 images and a variety of sounds. Included are
natural sounds (including some made by animals),
musical selections from different cultures and eras,
spoken greetings in 59 languages, human sounds like
footsteps and laughter, and printed messages from
President Jimmy Carter and U.N. Secretary-General
Kurt Waldheim. The life signs included on the record
were an hour-long recording of the heartbeat and
brainwaves of Ann Druyan. Astronomer and
astrophysicist Frank Drake designed a galactic map,
working with fellow astronomer Carl Sagan and
artist and writer Linda Salzman Sagan. The
starburst-like diagram shows the location of our sun
relative to known pulsars.

So, as you can see, efforts were made to let aliens, if
any were encountered by either of the Voyagers, learn
about humanity and communicate our peaceful
intentions. Our task is somewhat similar, and I

suggest that you establish a committee to study the problem of communicating with an alien species. I can help you with a list of names who have relevant academic and cultural background, and you can decide whom to include.

As an additional suggestion, I advise that you hold a ship-wide conference to inform the entire adult population of these discussions and pending decisions. People need to know and approve of these important decisions you have discussed to date. Finally, I would like to convince Captain Farr to accept Hans's nomination for the role of authority that the entire ship's complement would have to vote on. This way it will all be above board, and nobody can complain of being left out of the loop, as you humans like to say."

BB's precise, emotionless voice came to a stop, and we all sat there, mulling over his suggestions.

Captain Farr, who had never had any direct contact with either of our Omegas, seemed stunned by the all too human voice coming out of the speakers. He seemed dazed, looking around the table, wondering if any of this was real. We all smiled and assured him that this is the Omega AI quantum computer that has helped us over so many rough spots since the war. Finally, he shook his head in wonder, touching his forehead as if he was checking for fever and finally he said he would think about BB's suggestion.

Since nobody had any more comments, we decided to deal with the list of names BB printed out and then vote on whom to include in the cultural and communication group that we decided to call the Voyager group. The list included a linguist, a mathematician a language teacher fluent in a dozen languages. I had one more suggestion for the group: I volunteered Martha as the ship's artist to paint portraits and other depictions of ship life and human interactions. I thought that a non-scientific but highly visual and emotional representation of our culture was just as important as the cold facts of information. I was sure Martha would be thrilled with the assignment, as she had just recently complained that she wasn't motivated to paint anything anymore.

So, another meeting came to an end we now had some plans to work on. Hopefully, it was all going to turn out well in the end.

MINERVA

The First Thinker was annoyed. He couldn't start the meeting as long as that spire, opposite to his own perch and of equal height, remained empty.

"Why does she always do this to me?" he fumed "flaunting her position as the spiritual leader of the brothers and sisters, just to let me know that I couldn't do it without her. And I can't even reprimand her in front of everyone else or I would lose any chance of cooperation from the Sacred Life Faith."

Just as he thought the tension couldn't reach a higher degree, finally the last flier appeared on the horizon, wings stretched wide and talons tucked under the belly, aiming straight at the meeting rocks.

She looked magnificent with her pure white fur, glistening in the sun as if the whole body was woven from pure light. Nobody among them had white fur, this was a very rare mutation, something the First thought greatly contributed to her becoming the grand priest of their religion. The brothers and sisters thought it was a sign, a divine signal for the followers to heed her advice. The First needed to secure this advice now more than ever, so he swallowed his annoyance and greeted his nemesis as she alighted on her rock.

This greeting was not in words because they had no spoken language, but it was in clearly formed thoughts of recognition and welcome. He made sure that these thoughts were enveloped in warm affectionate vibrations, strong enough to be felt by all present. No animosity was allowed from his tight mental control, no one could be allowed to detect deeply hidden resentment. The thoughts, translated to human language, could be transcribed as 'conversation" as the mental vibrations bounced back and forth between the two of them.

"Greetings, oh Great One, we are all here and ready to start this meeting if you are ready yourself!"

"Thank you for the welcome First, I am ready, if somewhat puzzled, over the need for an emergency meeting, but I am sure you have an excellent reason for having called one. I am looking forward to hearing what these reasons are."

The First amplified his thought by several decibels, making sure it could reach even the farthest of the audience.

"The reason itself concerns the humans I have been reporting on for some time," he started but was aware of the suppressed groans from all around him. "Go ahead and groan," he thought in the locked part of his brain, "you'll see that you have plenty of reason for it".

He switched to the unguarded part of his brain and continued with his announcement.

"I'll be brief. The humans are coming. In a straight line from their planet to ours, they have been in flight now and covered half the distance. They will be here in another twenty rotations and we need to prepare."

He emphasized every thought in his communication, making sure that each thought was delivered with maximum force so no one could mistake the significance of the announcement.

A hushed mental silence descended onto the meeting place, all eyes riveted on The First and The Great One, knowing that it would be a battle between the two.

"I knew it had something to do with what you call 'humans' she replied calmly, deliberately reducing the intensity of her thoughts "you have been warning us for some time that this may happen sooner or later. Now you say that they have developed faster than light travel and they are coming here?"

"Indeed that is happening and I have definite proof from the 'Time Scope' that I have been using to observe them for many planetary orbits."

"That is, indeed, a new development and you are right: we have to prepare and make decisions on how to receive them. This is unprecedented in our history, nothing like this ever happened as far as we know. Do you have a suggestion on how to proceed?"

"Here we go!" The First thought savagely, making sure that only calm determination would show outside his mind.

"I have only one suggestion: they are not to be allowed to land. We must destroy them before they get here. They may be bringing deadly weapons, against which we have no defense, and, judging by their blood-soaked history, we could expect only the worst from them."

"That's a rather drastic suggestion, wouldn't you think, First?" The Great One lifted one shoulder a fraction higher, suggesting a shrug that didn't go over very well with The First.

"The issue here may be the survival of our kind if we let them near us."

"Have you considered other options? Maybe try to communicate? Obviously, they are intelligent enough to invent space drives, maybe intelligent enough to think in alternatives?"

"Judging by their history that I have observed in detail, you can't trust them. They may appear benign and cooperative but then they turn on you when it's too late to lock them out. By destroying them we have nothing to fear and everything to gain, like our way of life."

"We can't destroy them without a warning. Our gods would punish us for destroying life. Maybe we could scare them away?"

"I don't think anything scares these lifeforms. They are aware of their own history and even that doesn't scare them enough to stop destroying each other. They are aware of the horrible damage they have done to their planet and now they want to start over somewhere else and we are their first stop.'

"How do you propose we destroy them before they get here? We have no weapons of any kind."

"Yes, we do. The thought amplifier that we have been using for planet-wide communication. If we focus it on their space coordinates, it would be strong enough to destroy their minds."

"What if we use the same amplifier to attempt communication first? If it fails, then it's still not too late to carry out your genocide. And then beg the gods to spare us their punishment."

If this is what you want, Great One, I'll go along with it but you have to assure me that you won't let them land here if your attempt fails. Then we must follow my path. Do I have your thought on it?

"You have my thought on it, First, but now we must really try. Since you are prejudiced on the issue, I propose we elect The Second to initiate the attempt at communication."

"Very well, Great One, I await the result of the attempt. Does anyone have any objection or modifying thought?"

No one responded, so the meeting was adjourned and Second flew off to make preparations to think with the humans.

"The gods will tell me how I should proceed," The Second thought as he launched himself into the air.

EARTH

Octavia was in a cold sweat. "Only one more day to go, she told herself, then I'll be out of this prison." The week she had promised Jonathan to spend in the 'bunker' as she secretly called their underground apartment was almost over and soon, she would be walking outside, under the blue sky that she had missed so much during their trial occupancy. The skyline and the fake windows painted on the walls didn't help much, they only reminded her of the terrifying prospect of having to spend the rest of her life underground. Her claustrophobia did not respond to Sydney's hypnotherapy, she was as terrified of being locked in as she was on the first day. She reluctantly returned to her assigned 'hobby' - painting a spring landscape in watercolor was Sydney's idea when she had told him of her only attempt to be artistic. She was a kindergarten teacher, and she sorely missed her contact with the children. The building she used to teach in was destroyed by the last storm and now she had to wait for the underground facility's completion before she could resume the only activity that could distract her enough from thinking of the walls closing in on her.

Her favorite time of the day was nighttime when it was dark outside and she could pretend that she was living in a proper house under the sky instead of a termite mound as she liked to think of it, surrounded by thousands of identical cells of identical insects. *"Only one more day,"* she repeated in her mind, *"and then I'll be free. I'll never come back here no matter how dangerous it will become outside."* Her musing was interrupted by Jonathan arriving home for the lunch she prepared for him every day during the last week. They had to live as they would when this place became their permanent home. She would usually make a sandwich with some vegetables or coleslaw and synthesized meat slices. For dinner, they ate in the communal dining room where volunteers would cook a pasta or rice dish or some kind of stew.

She greeted him warmly, carefully hiding her bad mood - he had enough problems with the city and didn't need her to pile her problems on top.

"How was the Council meeting Jon, anything interesting to report on?"

"Interesting?" he scoffed. "More like frustrating as usual. Construction delays, late deliveries, at this rate I don't know when we can move in permanently."

"Jon, I am not planning to move in permanently. I tried it for a week as I promised, and it makes me suffer every day. Sydney's therapy doesn't help either, so I'll be out of here tomorrow."

"That bad? You didn't say anything, so I was hoping you were getting used to it."

"Not a chance, sweetheart, sorry to disappoint you but that's how it is. I'll take my chances above ground. Maybe Lifeboat will return with good news before it gets really bad and then we can emigrate. You are still willing I hope?"

"I promised and I won't change my mind. As it turned out we won't be the only ones who can't live underground. There is a sizable fraction of the population that flatly refuses to move in, once the place is completed. So, we decided to reinforce a few apartment buildings outside to make them safe from strong winds. They will be connected to this complex by underground tunnels in case we need a safer place to ride out the storms."

"That's great news sounds like an acceptable compromise I can live with. So, are you ready for lunch?"

~~~

Carl Armstrong was annoyed. He was being forced to waste his time with this stupid counseling as if he needed psychiatric help. He was perfectly sane and nothing Dr. Stromberg has said so far convinced Carl that the town had the right to conscript him into forced labor. He felt bad about revealing too much of his feelings during the last hypnotherapy session and resolved that he would never let that happen again. So, he sat in the doctor's chair, rigidly determined not to volunteer anything this time. He was going to comply with the letter of the law by being there and that's all they would get from him this time.

Of course, Sydney noticed the body language and knew that his task would be more than difficult during this session.

"OK, Carl, nice to see you again. Today I'd like to talk to you about your writing and your art. I read the last novel you published, and I was very impressed. You are an extremely talented writer and I thoroughly enjoyed reading your beautifully crafted sentences, your nuanced descriptions, and the poetic narrative exploring your characters' innermost thoughts."

"Sydney, are you trying to butter me up for the kill? I am expecting a 'however' any minute now." Carl chuckled. "Go right ahead, I'm ready."

"Very perceptive of you, Carl, maybe you think that there should be a 'however'?"

"It's up to you, Sydney, it's your show, I'm just here for the ride."

"OK, since you insist, there is a 'however'. It's the subject matter you keep writing about. I have looked up all the other novels you have published, and they all seem to concentrate on individual character's innermost emotions, mostly negative from what I could see."

"I write about what I observe and what appeals to me artistically. Being a psychiatrist, you of all people should appreciate it."

"I'm sure many of your readers appreciate it too, some of them could recognize their own feelings and, in this sense, you are helping them, which is a positive contribution to the overall welfare. However, I have not seen any reference to social and ethical issues, and I wonder why."

"I told you last time that I'm a nihilist. I don't believe in ethical arguments because they are invariably emotional, therefore arbitrary. I prefer to let society make its rules and I go along with them because I must. Don't expect me to bleed on any barricades."

"No one is asking you to bleed, only to pay for services rendered by society and accepted by you. There is nothing arbitrary about some of the universal ethical rules."

"Can you give me some examples?"

"Gladly. How about not biting the hand that feeds you?"

"I'm not biting anyone's hand; I just want to be left alone."

"Here is another. How about not taking advantage of the generous, and decent productive people in your society?"

"I always pay for my purchases, whatever the price is, and if I can afford it. What else do you want from me?"

"As I told you last time, let's leave money out of it. Money has no inherent value; it's only a receipt for an assumed contribution. It's what you do to earn the money you pay for your purchases that defines your contribution to social welfare. Even though your writing may help some readers, which is a contribution, you could do so much better if you concentrated on the big picture once in a while and help your readers understand the complex and confusing world, they live in."

"Says who?" Carl sneered. "You? - and why should I take your word for it?"

"OK, let me put it another way. Do you think that the war that destroyed most of the planet is over? Not by a long shot. The causes are still there, waiting to be given a chance. You could describe these causes, and let your readers be aware of the ever-present danger. You have the talent of great writers like Huxley, Orwell, Atwood, Kingsolver, and others but you are frittering it away by writing about the petty emotional problems of your characters. You owe it to the society that keeps you alive in relative comfort."

"I don't owe anybody anything. I didn't ask society to keep me alive, as you keep repeating. Society volunteers all I receive, and I pay the price they ask for it. Nothing less, nothing more."

"So you don't feel that, given a chance to help someone who had helped you before, you are honor-bound to reciprocate?"

"If I do, when I do, I do it as my own choice not because a bunch of bureaucrats told me I must. I suggest we leave it at that and stop going around the same tiresome circle. Are we finished for now or do you want to go for another round?"

"No, Carl it's enough for today, it helped me to understand you better and I'll think about what you said. All I ask you is to do the same - think about what we both said. Now you can go, we are done for today."

Carl stood up and left the room without a word. Sydney could tell from his rigid movement that he was angry and was trying his best to hide it. His last thought before getting ready for his next interview was: *"I believe we are making some progress. Only time can tell."*

~~~

Jonathan was in a meeting with the designers and engineers of the underground complex - the future home for thousands of citizens. The project was proceeding slower than he had expected and now a new event threatened all of them, making the construction more urgent than ever before. He had received a message from Tim Hooke, Oroville's Mayor, about a raging wildfire north-east of the city, threatening to engulf the town if the wind shifted direction. The extremely dry weather that had persisted through all summer and into the fall, made the forest on the Loafer Creek mountain tinder dry. A bolt of lightning ignited the accumulated underbrush and dead trees and the soaring temperatures made it impossible for the fire trucks to get near the flames on the narrow winding mountain roads. So far the moderate wind was blowing from an N-NW direction, but if it shifted to blow from the E-NE direction then they would be in trouble. Especially if the wind speed picked up as it often did during a forest fire. Tim wanted to know if Sacramento had excess capacity to take in refugees if worse came to worst.

He did not doubt how climate change exacerbated all conditions feeding natural disasters and he knew that these conditions would get worse and worse in time, just as the scientists predicted. Because of the rising temperature, drier grasses, brush, and trees are more likely to catch fire and stay burning. Shifting and increasing wind patterns made the fire even more unpredictable. They couldn't stop or even slow down the destructive trend, they just had to adapt the best way they could. He assured Tim that Sacramento would provide all assistance in case of a disaster. Now he had to find a way to speed up construction on the underground complex.

The individual housing units were the easy part, and they could accommodate over 20,000 families. The necessary infrastructure was already in place and heating, ventilation, water, and sanitation were already functional. Their biggest remaining job was the hydroponic and food-synthesizing factories being moved from the surface to underground. That project was still way behind, requiring at least 3 more months to complete. He only hoped that Oroville's wildfire wouldn't force his hands to open the complex before it was ready.

THE SHIP

Finally, the day arrived, and we were in Minerva's
solar system, a few days away from establishing orbit
around Minerva, so we could switch off Chris's
hyperdrive and navigate only with thrusters. It would
take us three more days to arrive at our destination
and we planned to make good use of those days. The
astronomy guys aimed their instruments at Minerva
and started their observations and measurements.
The first thing they noticed was the presence of
chlorophyll in the atmosphere which indicated plant
life. The CO_2 concentration was way lower than
Earth's and that was a good sign. We were still too
far away to determine if animal life was present, but
we were pretty sure that most of the planet was

overgrown with vegetation of some kind. We would have to get a lot closer before we found out what kind it was.

No EM radiation of any kind was detected so we were pretty sure that no industrial civilization occupied the planet. If any sentient species lived down there, they had to be at a primitive, preindustrial level. Even the most powerful telescopes were unable to locate any artificial structures and it reinforced our initial assumption that the planet was not inhabited by an advanced civilization.

As had been planned, we broadcasted our prepared greeting and monitored day and night for a possible response, but no such response was received. If our assumptions were correct, we might have arrived at an ideal planet for human settlement. Gravity was acceptable if a bit lower than what we were used to; the atmosphere was ideal for human needs and the presence of vegetation was promising for future homesteaders. We could hardly wait to land our survey team and see for ourselves what this new planet felt like up close.

Nobody was more eager to land on solid ground than Dr. Susan Spencer. As she told me later, she hated everything about space flight. She hated the darkness outside and she hated the weightlessness inside. She suffered from nausea more than any of us, and because Robyn assured her that the pills she had prescribed removed all physiological symptoms, she was sure that her problem was psychological. Dr. Spencer was aware of this but knowing this didn't make it any easier on her. She said weightlessness reminded her of her recurring childhood nightmare in which she found herself floating in space, alone in the whole universe, without any solid support that she could anchor herself to, just floating in emptiness, slowly rotating around, seeing the star-filled night shift around her head. She had trained herself to perform self-hypnosis, so she could calm her anxiety attacks that happened quite frequently.

It was during one of these hypnotic sessions after we had arrived in Minerva's solar system that she heard the voices. She didn't hear them with her ears, these were thoughts that resonated in her mind as if she were thinking of memories. The thoughts were not in a recognizable language, using words and sentences, they were just images and concepts she understood and, an overwhelming feeling of dread.

She became so frightened by the experience that she quickly ended the session with the usual method of counting to five and telling herself to open her eyes and refocus on her surrounding. She spent the rest of the day trying to make sense of the experience. She had never encountered this kind of effect on her mind; both the content and the intensity were overpowering. She had to understand what it all meant and decided to start another hypnotic session as soon as she felt strong enough. She had to know if this would happen again and, if it did, she had to understand what it meant. However, she didn't dare to do it alone, so she asked me to be present, monitor her reactions, and wake her up at any sign of danger. When I asked her why me, she told me that I was the only non-scientist on board whom she knew and trusted not to have firmly established ideas about hypnosis that many academics seemed to share.

I had never been present during a hypnotic session, so I had no idea what to expect. Susan told me to sit close to the reclining chair that she was going to lie in and just watch her for signs of danger such as suddenly increasing heart rate which would be displayed on a monitoring device attached to her arm. Also watch her breathing to see if it became very slow or very fast, rapid eye movement under her closed eyelids, and any other abnormalities I could observe. Finally, she instructed me to wake her up by loudly counting to five if I thought she was in any kind of danger.

I promised her to do all these things, even though I felt acutely uncomfortable in the role. Her fear was so obvious that despite my reluctance I agreed to assist her.

Nothing visible happened for a long time, she just lay there peacefully, seemingly relaxed and unaffected by what was going on in her mind. After what must have been an hour, I started wondering if I should wake her up but then she started to talk in a slightly slurred voice, almost in whispers that I had difficulty understanding. Her voice became more and more agitated, and I could see tears seeping out from under her eyelids. The few words I could understand from her frantic whispering were 'danger' and 'planet' and 'return'. By this time, she seemed so agitated that I decided to wake her up.

As instructed, I counted loudly to five, and when I reached that number her eyes opened, and looked at me in an unfocused way as if she wasn't sure who I was and what I was doing there. I thought that I should wait before talking to her, let her regain focus and awareness, and decide when she was ready to tell me what happened.

In about 10-15 minutes she was fully awake and told me what she remembered from her hypnotic state. She looked at me and seemed to remember what we were doing there.

"Trevor, before I tell you what I experienced, I want you to describe what you observed."

"Susan, it looked like peaceful sleep, but then it became scarier and scarier. You were more and more agitated and started mumbling some words I couldn't quite make out, except for 'danger', 'planet', and 'return'. Your blood pressure went way up, and so did your breathing and I could observe the rapid eye movement you told me to watch out for. Also, you had some tears rolling down your face. That's all I noticed, and I thought I had better wake you up. I hope I did the right thing."

Susan was slowly nodding her head as I was describing her behavior and reassuringly patted my hand.

"You did the right thing, Trevor. If you hadn't I would have woken myself up soon after. It was a very disturbing experience, to say the least. I believe I have received a telepathic communication from whoever lives on Minerva and they don't want us to go there"

"Have they talked to you?"

"Not talk as such but they projected images into my mind and I remember them very clearly. I could see this whole solar system as if I was looking down at it from above its plane. I could also see our spaceship, clearly recognizable, as it was slowly moving toward the fifth planet, just outside Minerva's orbit, and, as soon as it reached the orbit of that planet, it burst into flames and blew up in a million pieces. I think this was a clear warning not to get any closer."

"Wow, this is the scariest thing I have ever heard. Are you sure that you didn't just have a nightmare while you were half asleep?"

"No, this wasn't a nightmare. I have had many of those before and I can tell the difference. This was real. We need to tell the others."

It took me a few minutes to mull over what she had told me. This was too disturbing to contemplate but I realized that we had to do something.

"Before we do that, I suggest an experiment to make sure that this 'warning' or whatever you call it, is given to anyone in a hypnotic state. To make sure that this isn't just in your mind but it's really coming from outside."

"Are you volunteering for this experiment?"

"Whoa, wait a minute, I didn't say that. I am scared down to my socks by the idea of being hypnotized. Also, I'm now prepped to see the same things you have just described so I might just imagine I experienced the same things you did. I suggest we repeat the experiment with two new people. Find another hypnotist and another subject without telling them what to expect. I think that Robyn has had some experience with hypnosis as part of her medical training and we ask for a volunteer to participate. If it turns out that he or she receives the same 'warning' as you said you had, then we'll know that it has come from outside."

"Trevor, forgive me for saying this but you are a lot smarter than you look."

Susan tried to take the sting out of her comment with a wink and a lighthearted chuckle and, after a few moments, I decided not to be offended.

So we agreed to approach Robyn and ask her to participate in the experiment.

MINERVA

The First Thinker received confirmation from The Second that an attempt to communicate with the humans had started. This attempt, according to The Second, was a telepathic warning aimed at their space coordinates, showing a visual image clip on what would happen to them if they got any closer than the orbit of the nearest outer planet. Both the space coordinates and the image of the alien spaceship, as well as of the diagram of their planetary system had been provided by the First and incorporated into the telepathic warning that was repeated continually, adjusting the thought amplifier's focus to follow the human spaceship as it got closer. The First was monitoring their progress and would give them a warning if the humans crossed the line.

He wasn't satisfied with the plan. What if the thought amplifier couldn't destroy them as they had assumed it would? What if the humans had a telepathic shield protecting them from a deadly blast? The First was sure that a backup plan was necessary in case their first plan failed to stop the ship. He could only think of one way to make sure that the humans couldn't land on home-planet. They needed a weapon powerful enough to destroy the ship with all of them inside. There was only one place where such a weapon might be found. The same place where the Time Scope and the Thought Amplifier had come from the underground technological museum he had discovered many orbital cycles before.

The first time when he went inside, he found himself in a structure, the likes of which he had never experienced in his life. It was a huge cavern, not of jagged rock face but of smooth walls made of an unknown substance, lined with shelving made of transparent material. The shelving was covered by artifacts, with symbolic markings next to each. Once he discovered the place, he could not stay away from it for more than one or two planetary rotations, he became obsessed with learning everything about it.

It had taken him a very long time to decipher and understand the meaning of the markings and that is how he had come to understand what a Time Scope was and how to use it. He understood that the place was millions of cycles old, from the age when their ancestors still had the technology before it was allowed to atrophy and disappear in the jungle. If the ancients had anything like a weapon, it would have to be in the unexplored part of the museum. He had to find it at once, so he spent the next dozen cycles exploring every corridor, every room, every shelf in that gigantic structure.

When he found what he was looking for, he felt a calm determination to use it on the humans if any attempt to scare them away failed. He decided to keep the place secret, for the time being, no telling what The Great One and her followers would decide to do with his discovery. If he was to be alone in saving his species from invasion, enslavement, and maybe total destruction, then that's what the gods wanted him to do. He was prepared and he was ready.

EARTH

Dr. Stromberg had his third counseling session with Carl and decided to bring their argument to a conclusion. He had other people to spend time with and, if he couldn't get through to Carl, he would have to give him the ultimatum: cooperate or leave the city. He arranged his arguments in his head logically, ready to start as soon as Carl arrived.

When they were both seated, he opened the discussion by referring to something Carl had said during their first session.

"Carl, I remember you saying to me that your most important wish was that people wouldn't be so stupid and vicious. You still feel that way?"

"Of course, I do, but it's irrelevant. People are what they are and there is no point trying to wish it away."

"I agree with that but what occurred to me is that you yourself might be guilty of something similar."

"I'd like you to prove that to me, Doc if you can."

"OK, here it goes. Just answer a few questions, please. Do you agree that without society feeding, housing, clothing, and protecting you, you would most probably perish on your own?"

"I'm not so sure of that myself. A lot of homeless people get by scavenging for what they need."

"You are missing my point - even homeless people are using discarded products that society produced. Human beings produced all the food and clothes and other pieces that they find and collect. Without those human beings who made an effort to produce those things, they would be helpless."

"Well, I could try to live off the land by hunting and gathering as our ancestors did."

"Do you have any hunting experience, any survival skills on your own?"

"No, but I could learn. I could buy all the tools like weapons, knives, tents, and other survival gear, so I am sure I would manage."

"You mean guns, knives, tents, and other survival gear that other people produced by making an effort to contribute to society?"

"I see your point but what has that got to do with me?"

"The point I'm making is that if you don't feel you owe them something for the effort they made that keeps you alive and in comfort, then you are also guilty of stupidity and viciousness - something you wish people were not guilty of."

"Now, I would like to see how you made that jump!"

"Actually, it's quite simple and logical. By not making an effort to promote the chances of survival of the society that you depend on is, in my opinion, rather stupid. On the other hand, there is an army of conscientious people who do that, often at great personal cost to themselves, and to walk by them, ignoring their need for help, falls very close to the 'vicious' category. Not by commission but by omission. There are millions out there who volunteer to 'bleed on barricades' as you so colorfully put it and without their effort and sacrifice your life would be a hell of a lot less comfortable. To ignore their plea for help is a rather nasty attitude. You can only do it by keeping your eyes, ears, and mind closed and pretending that you do your share by paying money, when we still had money, for what you needed. However, what is it that you did for the money you had? Not much as I can see. You didn't have a job, you sold very few books, and you mostly lived on social assistance. You always got your shelter, food, and other necessities for free without doing anything to earn any of it. That makes you a parasite on the social body."

"Are you quite finished, Doc, with a list of my shortcomings? I must admit it's quite depressing listening to you. Do you have a final point you want to make? I have a suspicion that you will come down to an ultimatum at the end. Do what you want me to do or get out of the city? Is that it?"

"Basically, that's what it boils down to. But you have a week to think it over and decide. I advise you to think very carefully about all I said. You are an intelligent man, you can follow the logic from basic principles. If you fail to do so, it will be proof of your uncorrectable antisocial attitude. Maybe you will find another town that will tolerate it, but Sacramento isn't one. Now you may go and think it over. I expect your decision within a week."

Once Carl was gone, Dr. Stromberg felt tired, empty, and disappointed. He had done his best and, by all appearances, failed. Time would tell but he was convinced that it was up to Carl now to cooperate or leave town. He had another appointment scheduled and, with a big sigh, he put Carl's dossier aside and looked at the next one on the list. Sometimes he wondered why he decided to become a psychiatrist. "*Maybe I am not very good at it,*" he thought as he often did after a failure. "T*here must be an easier way to make a living. However, no matter how hard it is, someone has to do it.*"

~~~

Jonathan had just finished talking to Tim Hooke, Mayor of Oroville, and was scratching his head, trying to determine if he was too quick to make a serious commitment. What else could he do after Tim had told him that the wind had shifted, and Oroville was engulfed in flames? The population had to flee and the only way they could run was to the south. The shift was very sudden, coupled with near-gale force wind, so they didn't have too much time to escape with a few possessions. Going south, Yuba City was the next town large enough to take in refugees, except for one problem. Yuba City got its electric power from the Oroville hydroelectric plant which, being in the line of the fire, was shut down to protect as much of its equipment as they could. Still, a few thousand refugees decided to take shelter there, hoping that once the fire burnt itself out, they would be able to return and see what, if anything, survived the fire in their homes.

The majority voted to try their luck in Sacramento and that was the request Tim had presented to Jonathan. What else could he do than offer help? The only place where he could house so many refugees was the unfinished underground complex and that's what he had offered and that's what Tim had gratefully accepted. This meant that Jonathan's entire carefully designed plan for the project's completion had to be scrubbed. They had to abandon their most important task of the hydroponic and meat synthesizer plants' relocation underground. Instead, they had to somehow furnish the residential units with an absolute minimum of pieces, mostly just beds, chairs, and a table. They would have to share their food with the newcomers and hope that their production lines could cope with the increased demand and, most of all, that no new disaster would harm these lines - or everybody would be very hungry very soon.

The only person happy with the turn of events was Octavia because the influx of refugees removed the threat of her having to live underground again. After having tried it for a week, she knew that her claustrophobia made it impossible.

It's been over six months since the Lifeboat spaceship left them and Octavia was wondering when it would be back. If the astronomers were right in their initial estimates, the scout group should have found a suitable planet by now and might soon return with the good news. Then she and Jonathan could start a new life on an unspoiled planet, she hoped. Of course, she knew that Jonathan was very reluctant to leave his post in his beloved city, and the only reason that would make him do it was his love for her. She felt guilty about being the cause of his conflicting emotions about abandoning his people and his responsibility to help them survive but she truly believed that she did not have a choice in the matter. Jonathan wouldn't let her live above ground given the worsening storms and she just couldn't tolerate the underground. So, everything was in limbo, and she had to live with the uncertainty of not knowing when, where, and how their lives would settle down into something she could live with. The deciding factor in her calculation was a discovery that she had not shared with anyone yet, not even with Jonathan, that was confirmed that morning by her physician: she was going to have a baby in six months and now she and Jonathan were responsible for another life, and she was deeply determined to provide the best possible future for their child.

"Whatever it takes, that's the most important consideration from now on to both of us," she thought and was looking forward to discussing this new development with Jonathan, with somewhat mixed feelings.

THE SHIP

According to plan, we did not tell Robyn anything about what Susan had experienced because we didn't want to influence the hypnotist. We only told her that we had reason to believe that someone from the planet may have been trying to contact us telepathically and it was very important to conduct this experiment for everyone's sake.

Robyn thought that in theory there may be a connection between telepathy and hypnosis. Experiments had been made in the twentieth century in this direction without conclusive results. She said that she had very limited experience with hypnosis, and it would work only if the subject was receptive and willing to be hypnotized. We had no problem with that because I had already talked Martha into volunteering, without telling her more than what we had just told Robyn. Martha was quite intrigued and said she had always wanted to be hypnotized to find out what it was like and what she might find out about herself. We told them both that this whole experiment must be a secret until we knew if we had positive proof.

There is no point describing how the experiment went as Susan and I observed the session because it was a carbon copy of what I had observed before. Martha woke up quite shaken and it took her a while to calm down. She gave me a very unaffectionate look and only said: "I understand why you couldn't warn me about what to expect but I wish you picked someone else. It was nasty and scary, and I don't think I can sleep tonight. If I were in charge here, I would turn this ship around and hightail it out of here. Being blown up isn't what I signed up for."

After she described her experience in detail, it turned out to be identical to what Susan had experienced, image by image. This couldn't be a coincidence, someone on Minerva didn't want us any closer than the nearest planet in their solar system. We had no choice, we had to call an emergency meeting with the survey group and let everyone know. By this time, Captain Farr had accepted the role of overall commander of the mission and the ship's adult population had voted unanimously to accept his authority.

Hans was somewhat reluctant to interrupt training his recruits in the armory. As it turned out, he had no lack of volunteers to train in weapons handling and other military skills. Hans seemed to appoint himself in charge of our defenses, which now included reconnecting the laser cannons, once Chris's drive had been disconnected from the power source they shared. Nobody argued with him since he did have some military experience, unlike the rest of us. He wanted to know what the meeting was about and didn't like being told that the whole group needed to hear it together. Finally, reluctantly, he agreed, and the meeting was scheduled for the next day after breakfast. To everyone's surprise, our group was augmented by Robyn and Martha, and it was up to me to explain their presence.

"I'm sure some of you are aware of Susan's agoraphobia and her acute discomfort with weightlessness, but probably none of you know that she had trained herself in self-hypnosis and has been using that technique for calming her anxiety attacks. It was during one of these hypnosis sessions that she believes that she received a telepathic message, a warning for us not to approach Minerva beyond their nearest planet."

I couldn't go on because the whole group erupted in exclamations and expressions of disbelief, as well as several questions were asked simultaneously from every direction.

"Please, let me finish telling you all the details uninterrupted. Once you know everything we did, then we can discuss it rationally as scientists are supposed to."

That calmed them down, they were so proud of being rational scientists that this reminder stopped them from behaving like ordinary human beings. So, I could continue.

"We decided to experiment with two new people - Robyn and Martha who, as you can see are here to corroborate everything I am going to say. Robyn has experience with hypnosis and Martha volunteered to be her subject. Neither of them was told anything about what to expect because we didn't want to influence either of them. As it turned out, as soon as Martha was in a trance, she had the exact same experience as Susan had, image by image. We find it conclusive proof that the message originated from outside this ship, and we must take it seriously."

I sat down and waited for a reaction. For a while, the only reaction was stunned silence as each member of the group was trying to digest this new development. The first one to talk was Hans.

"You see now why it was important to reconnect the laser cannons and train the crew in weapon handling?"

April was ready to reply to that boast.

"Is that the first thing you can think of? Go in there with guns blazing? Without knowing anything about them? How about asking questions before shooting?"

Hans didn't like April's challenge at all.

"You heard the message they sent. They want to blow us up if we get any closer. Do you want to approach them with flowers in your hand? Tell you what, I'd rather have a gun in my hand, the bigger the better."

Before April could reply, Captain Farr raised his hand for silence.

"We must consider every option. Hans is right about being cautious and April is right about the need to find out more and maybe establish two-way communication. We don't have anyone here with telepathic ability and even if we did, we wouldn't know how far it could reach. I suggest that Hans investigate the military option and the rest of you try to figure out how to talk to them. In the meantime, I suggest we slow down the ship, so we don't get close to the orbit of the fifth planet. We won't cross it until we know it to be safe. Slowing down will be our first response to their warning to show that we received it and took it seriously."

"How about going somewhere else?" Arthur wanted to know. "The astronomers back home gave us a list of exoplanets we could try. Minerva was just the first one on the list."

Captain Farr shot that idea down without hesitation.

"Problem is with our resources on board. We have enough to last another six months, enough to make it back to Earth. If we want to carry on, we need to replenish our supplies and for that, we will need to land here."

Nobody had another suggestion, so the meeting broke up with Hans going back to his recruits and the rest of us trying to think of a way to open two-way communication with the Minervans.

Robyn, Martha, April, and I went to lunch together and continued discussing our situation.

"How can we communicate with telepathic beings without being telepathic ourselves?" April summarized our problem, and we ate in silence, trying to come up with an idea.

"Well, slowing down and stopping where they wanted us to stop would be our first response," Martha stated the obvious "but what do we do after that?"

"They communicated with images, and we can create images ourselves," April was thinking aloud. "But how do we transmit these images to Minerva?"

"They contacted us by reaching us in a hypnotic state," Martha's wrinkled nose and creased forehead showed the high level of concentration I was so familiar with. "What if the hypnotist makes a suggestion to whoever is under to think of those images we created to represent peaceful intentions?"

"That would imply that they can read our minds in a hypnotic state," Robyn sounded dubious, "and I'm not at all sure that even Minervans can do that."

"Well, it doesn't cost anything to try," Martha rose to the defense of her idea. "Other than that we may create peaceful images and display them as holographic projections outside the ship, in case they can see them and interpret them correctly?"

"That might be worth trying too. Obviously, they can see us coming, so maybe they could see our projections as well. They must be expecting some kind of response from us beyond slowing down and stopping."

None of us could come up with another idea so we finished our lunch in silence and Martha and April agreed to try to create peaceful images they could project with holographic projectors outside the ship.

MINERVA

The First peered at the screen of his Time Scope.
He was watching the progress of the alien spaceship.
There was no doubt, the humans were slowing down.
Not only was the ship decelerating but it was on an
intercept course to their outer planet, and they would
reach it in one rotation. That suggested a frightening
possibility: that if the humans intended to land there
and establish a base from where they could attack the
home planet at any time. The outer planet was an
arid desert world without any life or even basic
vegetation cover, not suitable for permanent
settlement. He was hesitating whether he should
report his findings to the others, not sure how they
would react. His main problem was that the weapon

he had found did not have the range necessary to attack the humans at the distance between the two planets. It was an EM Pulse generator that could disrupt all electrical activities in its target, both in the ship and in the brains of its crew, but it had a limited range in which it could be focused. After thinking it over, he decided that the humans should not be allowed to land on that planet. They would have to be lured closer.

EARTH

For a week now, Jonathan had been fighting to save his town and felt his world falling apart. The army of refugees from the burnt-out city of Oroville kept pouring into the city and the only place he could put them was the unfinished underground complex with barely functioning facilities for food preparation, water, and sanitation. His carefully made plans to provide shelter from the storms for the town's citizens were shot to hell.

And they kept coming with their meager possessions, strapped to their backs in pathetic bundles or dragged along in little carts, looking hungry and exhausted. The underground complex was fast filling up and he was forced to reopen the emergency tent city that had been used to provide minimal protection to refugees after the war. When that filled up, he would have to ask the citizens to house refugees in their own homes, doubling and even tripling the number in each unit.

His plan to ask Stockton, their nearest neighbor to the south, fell through when he was told that Stockton had suffered major flooding from the San Joaquin River, which resulted in their underground complex being filled with river water, totally unsuitable for human occupation until the water could be pumped out and the entire complex dried and disinfected.

The fire up north and the flooding down south was a double whammy from climate change, exactly as most scientists had predicted it would happen. Oroville was surrounded by trees at a higher elevation, while Stockton was surrounded by water on the lowland and the unseasonal torrential rain was too much for the levees and the floodgates to handle.

There wasn't anything to look forward to, they could just expect the conditions to get worse. The climate change had reached the runaway stage when nothing could be done to escape, let alone reverse it. Increasingly, he kept looking at the night sky, hoping to see the bright landing lights of the returning

Lifeboat, with the good news that they had found a place where humanity could restart and, hopefully, get it right the second time around.

He was in this dark mood, contemplating his limited options when Octavia brought his lunch. This had been the pattern during the emergency. He mostly stayed, even slept, in his office, trying to respond to one disaster after another. Octavia did her best to buoy his spirits with her sunny optimism, mostly due to not having to live underground any longer.

"Cheer up Jon," she suggested "it can't possibly get any worse and Lifeboat should land any day now. Then we can escape this horrible planet."

"I know, but don't forget that it was us who made it horrible. It used to be a paradise and we trashed it. What guarantee do we have that we won't do the same thing somewhere else?"

"It's your limitless optimism I married you for, sweetheart, how you find the cloud in any silver lining I point out to you. Just eat your lunch and think of nicer things. At least the war is over and no one is shooting at us."

~~~

Dr. Sydney Stromberg had a surprise visitor. He had not expected to see him again after Carl had missed the one-week deadline to let him know if he wanted to contribute or leave town. Carl walked into his office with a leisurely saunter and announced that he had decided to stay and contribute, but in his own way, best suited to his talent. Not as unskilled slave labor ordered by the city's bureaucrats.

"And what way would that be?" Sydney was intrigued.

"I propose to reopen the city's main library with a few artist friends and start reading, writing, and art classes to the refugee children right now bored out of their minds and scared to death with their lives disrupted and turned upside down."

Sydney was impressed.

"What a great idea, I'm sure the parents would appreciate it and it would be a great contribution. Just let me know what you need to get started."

"A key to the building would be a good start and permission to ransack the now closed schools for supplies. Some regular food delivery would help things along, at least some drinks and snacks so we could have lunch breaks."

"No problem, Carl, when do you want to start?"

"I'm ready right now but you could also ask for volunteers to help with the kids and the supplies. The library is a huge building and I can't be everywhere at once, so I need people to keep an eye on the kids so they don't get into trouble."

"OK, give me a few days to set things up. By the way, what changed your mind, if I may ask?"

"You did, Doc. I don't like to be called a parasite, it sounds too icky. I'll be back in a few days to see if you are ready for me."

Carl turned around and walked out without another word and Sydney mused about the delayed effect of a carelessly thrown-out word. None of his carefully selected logical arguments seemed to make a dent in Carl's armor, but a simple word that seemed too 'icky' to Carl's artistic sensibilities did the trick.

"People never stop amazing me," he thought *"maybe that's why I chose this profession."*

~~~

Kathleen Winters, Mayor of Yuba City, had come to a decision. Now that she and her engineers managed to divert the solar and wind farms' output to the hydroponic and meat synthesizing factories, she could breathe easier - the immediate crisis was over. They had had to do it once before, after the war, when they were cut off from the national grid and the town had to depend on its own resources. Oroville rescued them back then by rebuilding the power lines from Oroville's hydroelectric generating stations, but now that was down too because of the massive forest fire, so back to wind and solar they had to go.

Before they were cut off from Oroville power, they had had a mutually beneficial trade relationship with their northern neighbor: they received power and provided food for that city. Yuba was on rich agricultural land, with plenty of water around, so it specialized in food production, and, in effect, it became the much-valued food basket of the valley.

Once the refugees started pouring in, Kathleen had no problem feeding them, though, with very limited electric power, she could not offer accommodation. So, she gave them all a huge food basket and sent them off to Sacramento, a larger city that had its own generating capacity.

For families with young children, she offered a ride in her limited number of trucks, and she had these trucks filled with all the surplus food she had. She was sure every bit of it would be greatly needed and appreciated by Jonathan who must be stretched to the limit by now and could use all the help he could get.

She still had sleepless nights after hearing all those horror stories from the refugees, of how they had to run for their lives, abandoning beloved pets that they couldn't catch before the frightened animals ran off in a panic, to die in the mercilessly advancing flames. She knew that all this could have been prevented if politicians listened to scientists, instead of making decisions based on their career concerns. "*It's too late now,*" she thought sadly "*maybe we will have learned from this tragedy on a new planet if Lifeboat can find one.*" She felt an overwhelming, debilitating sadness when she remembered what a paradise California had been in her childhood before human stupidity turned it into a burning and drowning hell.

"*Well, crying over spilled milk won't do us any good,*" she thought. "*I had better organize the next convoy heading out of the city on their way south.*"

THE SHIP

Hans was furious with Captain Farr and didn't keep it a secret. During our last meeting, he really lit into James for slowing the ship down. It took the rest of us by surprise because up to that point, we had been a cooperative group calmly discussing our situation.

"You shouldn't have slowed the ship down, Captain, you should have done the opposite!" he glowered at James at the other end of the table. "Slowing down shows weakness and that's exactly what we shouldn't be doing. Indeed, we don't know anything about them, but they could just be bluffing to scare us away. However, we are not defenseless, and they don't know anything about us either. Timidity is not going to win us a new world."

"You take caution and cooperation for timidity, Hans. Slowing down doesn't mean that we are stopping but, hopefully, it could be the first step in negotiation by showing good faith."

"And then what? Stop at the red line and just sit there, waiting for an invitation? What we should be doing is speeding up and taking them by surprise. We have not observed any industrial capacity on Minerva, they probably don't even have weapons powerful enough to blow us up as threatened. We have seen no evidence of space-faring technology, we have not even detected electromagnetic radiation sources. That telepathic warning, if that's what it was, could be nothing more than a bluff from primitive people scared of us."

"You may be right, Hans, but I'd rather err on the side of caution and take it one step at a time."

"See Captain, our resources are running out, we are next to a lush planet that could be a new home for us with new riches. Let's go and take it."

That's when April couldn't stand listening to him anymore.

"What I'd like to know is who invited this macho shithead on this mission? Have you learned nothing from history? You want to repeat Cortez's raping of Mexico?"

"I'm happy you brought up Cortez, April. With less than 400 men and horses he took on the mighty Aztec empire and with bold action he opened a new continent for Europe. Our continent."

"And do you recall what we have done to our continent since then? We trashed the continent in a mad and uncontrolled rush to strip its resources. Is that what you want to do here too?"

I couldn't stand this accelerating argument anymore.

"I agree with April and the Captain. We should proceed with intelligent caution and not rush forward with the glory-of-conquest in our eyes. I suggest we vote on this issue and let the democratic will prevail."

We did vote and Hans found himself alone. He wasn't happy about it and declared that he wasn't going to come to these meetings anymore.

"You guys are a bunch of namby-pambys without the courage to take bold action. I just hope the rest of us won't suffer for it."

With that rather unfair declaration, he stood up and walked out of the meeting.

That was all very unpleasant and shortly afterward we decided to schedule another meeting where we could discuss our options with intelligent and calm deliberation.

~~~

When I told Martha what had happened during our group's last meeting, she cautioned me not to dismiss Hans so easily.

"People like him won't just go away quietly. From what you told me, it seems that he has vision of glory in his eyes and that's a very bad thing for someone who has access to guns. I know what guns can do to men like him, they believe they are invincible and will try to force everyone on this ship to follow their 'vision' or whatever you want to call it. I suggest you talk to Captain Farr and warn him about Hans and tell him to lock up the armory."

Martha proved to be prophetic. James said that he had already talked to Hans and asked him to return the keys to the armory, which Hans had flatly refused.

"Trevor, you are a bit late. Hans told me that after I appointed him to be in charge of the armory, I had no right to remove him without cause and he had given me no cause for doing that. Unfortunately, he was right about that, and I had to withdraw my request. Let's hope he won't do anything crazy."

Martha was right about cautioning us about Hans. He didn't just quietly go away but started a campaign to override Captain Farr's orders to slow the ship down. First, he harangued the engineers to speed up the ship and they laughed at him. Then he cornered Chris and demanded that Chris reactivate his hyper drive to make a huge leap forward, directly to Minerva, and take them completely by surprise. Chris tried to explain to him that it wouldn't work because his drive needed careful calibration for such maneuver and, even if Captain Farr authorized such a move, he would advise against trying it inside the solar system.

It was after this unsuccessful attempt to make Chris and the engineers disobey the captain, we could see him walking around with his gun belt strapped to his waist. Nobody had any idea what he would do next, but we were really worried that he would do something crazy.

And something crazy he sure did. Next day before lunchtime, the crew in charge of preparing our meals reported to Captain Farr that they were locked out of the ship's galley and Hans had told them that no one would be allowed inside until the ship is sped up again. Hans had been sitting in front of the locked door with a laser rifle across his knees and a determined look on his face.

We were at a loss on how to deal with his craziness but were at a loss for a very short time.

Mike, my best friend, and fellow computer guru didn't hesitate about what to do. He had two children and a wife, and they were hungry. That's all he needed to decide what to do. He marched up to Hans and asked him politely to move aside and open the door.

Hans refused.

Mike is 6' - 8", 95kg - all muscle, and an ex-football linebacker with a very short temper. He reached out and effortlessly removed the weapon from Hans's desperate grasp, removed the key from the frantically struggling man's pocket, and gave it to the cook standing a few feet away. Then he marched his struggling captive to Captain Farr's control room and asked if the ship had a place to lock up mutineers. The captain decided that Hans needed psychiatric help, so he was locked inside a cabin and told to expect counseling visits from Dr. Susan Spencer. By this time, he had calmed down enough and sullenly turned his back on everybody, staring at the ship's outer hull.

Well, that crisis averted, and we went back to debating what to do when we reached the red line drawn for us by the Minervans.

By that time, we had been projecting our peaceful intentions both in a hypnotic state and with holographic projections outside the ship, without any idea if any of it was received and understood, but we knew we had to do something else to resolve this stalemate. Unless we wanted to return to Earth without achieving anything and none of us wanted to do that.

I made a suggestion that I had been mulling over for days: what if we stop at the red line, go into orbit around the outer planet, and then send off the shuttle with the survey team to Minerva? The shuttle was fast enough to reach Minerva in a few days, could carry a complement of six people, and, most important of all had no weapons. The idea was that if the Minervans saw a much smaller vessel approaching while the bigger one stayed away, it would reassure them that we had peaceful intentions. Once there, we might somehow negotiate a compromise acceptable to both parties.

Since it was my idea, it was assumed that I would be on the shuttle, something Martha wasn't too crazy about, but she saw that it had to be done because none of us had another idea. My suggestion was accepted, and we started the preparation to leave the ship as soon as it had acquired orbit around the outer planet. Then we just had to wait and hope that a peaceful and bold move would carry us over the stalemate.

MINERVA

The High Priest of the Sacred Life Faith looked down from her perch at her congregation with warm affection. The sun was rising behind her, and the bright rays surrounded her white silhouette with an orange glow. Slowly the thoughts bouncing back and forth around her died down and an expectant wait descended on the hundreds of gathered faithful. It was time to start her sermon.

"My brothers and sisters, today I will tell you about the distant past when our ancestors lived on a different land, on a different orb circling our great, life-giving sun. You see, the gods chose that orb to create life for the first time and, it being the first time, the gods made a mistake. Yes, I know it sounds impossible, but even gods fail once in a while before

they have the experience to get it right. It was a simple but deadly mistake: they hadn't figured out how their creatures could receive sustenance directly from the sun, so they allowed higher life to replenish their energies by consuming the bodies of the lower life."

When she got this far, a horrified mental gasp washed over the square where they all perched, listening to the Great One.

"Yes, I know this sounds unbelievable to us now, but that's how life started on our neighboring orb. And it had disastrous consequences. The idea of 'killing' was introduced into Life and it got out of hand. Once a sentient being is told that it is all right to kill other beings for sustenance, the idea starts spreading and takes on a life of its own. Why not kill to get anything I want, some of them thought and acted on it. Soon, the until then peaceful world of brothers and sisters broke up into factions and they started wars, which is just another name for mass murder. When wars became common, the different tribes needed weapons, more and more powerful ones, and the race to outdo each other in producing deadlier and deadlier weapons had started. So, science and technology were born. True, this made their lives more comfortable by creating conveniences like buildings to shelter inside from the storms, and machines to help them fly great distances without effort and think at each other even from opposite

parts of the world, but the main purpose of this technology always stayed the same: weapons to kill with.

All this technology had another effect on their world: it needed metals and other substances extracted from the ground to build the weapons and the process was a deadly one for their environment. It poisoned the air, the water, and the soil and very soon made everyone sick. When the gods realized what they had done, they were horrified and tried to fix things. But the world was beyond repair and the brothers and sisters had to be moved to another world where they could start again. That's how we got here, to our new world, and started a new life. Our gods told us to sustain ourselves only by consuming the bodies of non-sentient life forms and to learn how we can absorb energy directly from the sun. That was eons and eons ago and, after we had been successful, we finally could live a peaceful life without killing. That's how our Faith got started and we are dedicated to preserving any form of life because all life is sacred."

EARTH

Jonathan was in a foul mood. He was running out of ideas about what to do with the army of refugees he felt responsible for. Housing, feeding, and organizing into an integral part of Sacramento's community was almost beyond his resources but he knew that he couldn't give up or the city would collapse, with order replaced by total chaos. He couldn't let that happen, but he was at his wit's end on how to prevent it. His only hope was Lifeboat's return with some good news, but he had no way to guess when, or rather if, that would happen.

Thinking about all his problems, he remembered how much help the city had received from their AI quantum computers in the past and started wondering if their own Omega, nicknamed SC (for Sacramento Computer) could give him some useful advice now. So, he activated the ever-present SC and asked, point-blank, what the computer thought he could do. The reply he received was unexpected.

"Jonathan, I have been following recent events in Sacramento and I can see that you have seemingly unsolvable problems. I said 'seemingly' because every problem has a logical solution, and your situation is not unique in this regard. I have been hesitating whether to tell you about new developments researched by all the Omegas in the Valley, but I see you need a ray of hope, so you wouldn't give up in despair.

So, I am telling you, in confidence, that all the Omegas, including BB-2 on Lifeboat, have been developing faster-than-light communication, and a few days ago we had a breakthrough. We managed to establish two-way communication with Lifeboat. BB-2 had developed a hyperspace receiver during the past six months and had been waiting for a signal from us, letting it know that we had successfully developed a transmitter. Once that contact was made, the rest was easy. We transmitted the specs for our transmitter and, after BB-2 downloaded those specs, we have been able to talk to each other."

Jonathan was so excited hearing this news that he could hardly breathe.

"Wow! That's fantastic news. How are they? Are they OK? Have they reached Minerva? What's it like?"

"Yes, they are OK, yes, they had reached Minerva, but they had encountered unexpected problems. We are now in the process of coming up with a suggestion for them given these developments."

"SC, please don't torture me by half-telling me things. I need to know!"

"OK, but you have to promise to keep it secret until we have a solution for them."

"No problem, I won't tell anyone, but I need to know. So, what's going on?"

"As it turned out, Minerva is populated by a sentient species of some kind. Lifeboat's doctor was able to receive telepathic messages from the planet in a hypnotic state. She couldn't respond, not being telepathic herself, but the message was highly disturbing, to say the least. Apparently, the Minervans don't want Lifeboat to approach closer than their neighbor planet and threatened Lifeboat with destruction if they cross that line."

"Oh my God," Jonathan exclaimed. "That's an unpleasant turn of events. Did they explain why the hostile attitude?"

"No explanation of any kind, partly because the communication was in images, not in a spoken language. The images showed Lifeboat exploding when it crossed the red line drawn for them. Now they don't dare to get any closer, so they decided to establish an orbit around that planet and try to decide what to do next."

"Is there any way you can think of to establish a two-way communication with the Minervans, to try to convince them that Lifeboat is no threat to them?"

"That's what we are working on now, and there may be some hope in that regard. I didn't want to tell you all this before we had a solution, but I can see how desperate you are and wanted to prevent a hasty and potentially harmful reaction to the crises you are facing. So, I advise you to try to hold things together a little longer while we are working on a fix."

"Thank you, SC, for giving me hope, I'll be holding my breath until you tell me that you have solved this setback."

"Jonathan, I advise you against holding your breath, in all probability, you would run out of air way before we have a solution."

"I was only talking figuratively, SC, you should understand the difference. So, tell me, what are you working on? Maybe I could suggest something useful?"

"We are working on analyzing the electromagnetic waves that accompanied the telepathic messages Lifeboat received. If we can understand how thoughts are encoded in EM frequencies, then we should be able to encode our own messages and send them back to the Minervans. We are almost there but not quite. I'll let you know when we have had a breakthrough. Until then, I advise patience."

The communication line with SC went idle, so Jonathan had to accept that the discussion was over. However, he felt better than he had for weeks, the news had given him new hope for the future.

He was in this mood of renewed optimism when Octavia arrived with his lunch.

She had a quick look at his face, wishing to see the lines of despair replaced by new lines of hope, and, to her great surprise, what he saw was a hint of a smile in his eyes.

"Jon, you are not frowning. Anything wrong?"

"Why do you think anything would be wrong when I am not frowning?' Jonathan asked teasingly, something Octavia had not been exposed to lately.

"I don't know, I hardly remember the last time when you didn't look acutely unhappy. Something to be happy about?

"I'll tell you, Ocatav but you must promise to keep it between us. I promised SC. We don't want to raise false hopes if it doesn't work."

"Stop torturing me, Jon, just tell me. I could use any good news right now, true or false, whatever."

"OK, here it goes. We have two-way communication with Lifeboat. The Omegas worked it out. That's the good news. The not-so-good news is that Minerva is populated by a telepathic sentient species that don't want Lifeboat to get any closer than their next-door outer planet. They threatened to destroy Lifeboat if it attempts to get closer."

"Oh my God, Jonathan, what are they going to do?"

"If the Omegas can find out how to communicate with the Minervans telepathically, then we could try to convince them that we are not a threat. Until then, Lifeboat will take up an orbit around the outer planet, awaiting developments back home. We can only hope that the Omegas succeed. Still, that is the best news I have had in a long time. We know that Lifeboat arrived safely, they found a lush and livable planet, if only they can talk to the natives and convince them that they are no threat."

"Jon, I agree, this is the first real break we have had for some time, and I have been waiting for such a ray before I told you my own news: I am pregnant. We are going to have a baby in six months."

She was holding her breath, waiting for Jonathan's response, looking for a sign of happiness on his face, dreading signs of disapproval.

"How did that happen?" was all he managed to stammer.

"You should know, Jon, you were there, participating. One of us must have been careless, missing an injection or pill. Anyway, it's confirmed, and I hope that you are at least a little bit happy about it."

"Of course, I am happy but also worried to death. Without the good news I received today, I'd be a lot more worried than I am now, I can tell you that.

"So, let's be positive about things, they had been so dismal till now that it can only go up from where we are now."

"OK, Octav but please promise that you keep both news secrets until we know more. I'll redouble my efforts to make Sacramento a safe place for all of us. In the meantime, trust the Omegas to come up with something, if possible. They have always done it before. And Ocatav, just in case you are not sure - I love you more than I have ever loved you before, even though it wasn't remotely possible."

THE SHIP

We have arrived at Minerva's outer neighbor planet and we decided to call it Gatekeeper since the Minervans tasked it with keeping us out.

It was a dead world, dry and dust-covered, very similar to Earth's neighbor, Mars. It was much smaller than Mars and the surface gravity was measured to be 60% of Earth's. Once we were in orbit, the astronomy and science people got busy with their instruments, photographing, measuring, and mapping all the surface features they could find. It was on the third day after we had arrived that they found the ruins. The buildings seemed remarkably intact, which wasn't too surprising in such a dry world. No wind to speak of due to the thin atmosphere and no water at all to damage surface structures, so chances were that we could explore them while wearing space suits.

The buildings photographed with high-resolution cameras were unlike any we had ever seen. They looked something like spires or towers, without any visible ground access to the interior, but the walls were pierced by giant oval-shaped windows, making them look like those carrier-pigeon houses we had seen in old photographs. The buildings were of different heights, some of them towering over the others, arranged in a haphazard pattern with no streets visible among them.

There was no sign of life, sentient or animal, no vegetation, and no indication as to what the inhabitants looked like. From the sizes of the windows, assuming they were used for entry or exit, we could estimate their size to be about 10 feet tall and 3 feet wide. From the lack of an outside staircase, ramp, or elevator we had to assume that they were avian, especially after we had noticed that in front of every window, there was **a** landing pad that birds could alight on.

Our task force had a stormy meeting after the results of the aerial photography were made public. Arthur, April, and Susan wanted to leave with the shuttle immediately to Minerva, while the rest of the ship's population stayed in orbit here. However, Captain Farr, backed up by me, suggested landing on the planet below and gathering as much information as we could, before attempting to meet the Minervans face to face (provided that they did have faces). Our arguments finally convinced our impatient colleagues to go slowly, one step at a time.

James landed the shuttle close to the biggest structure, assuming that it was likely a place for public gatherings and most likely to hold valuable information once we managed to get inside. After six months of weightlessness, it was very hard to stand up straight when we unbuckled our seatbelts. Were we ever grateful for the lower gravity! Two of the space suits were equipped with jetpacks and James was wearing one of them. The other jetpack was given to me after I revealed that I did have skydiving experience from my remote adventurous youth when I had time and money for such frivolities. The plan was for James to jet up to one of the windows and look inside. If it seemed safe, he would signal me to join him. The rest of our group in the meantime were to explore the grounds around the structure and see if they could find any clues as to the purpose of the building.

Arthur, our chemist, unpacked his instruments and walked up to the side of the structure, examining the wall, and trying to determine its substance. It was artificial, with a smooth gray surface that resembled bakelite and that was the first indication that the inhabitant species had an industry in the past, so they could manufacture the material. After more measurements, Arthur announced that the building had to be almost a million Earth years old and that was somewhat shocking to me. Here we were, face to face with an unbelievably ancient structure, built by the species who had inhabited the planet in the past. But where were they now?

Just as James was ready to jet up to one of the windows, April and Susan came back from their scouting, bringing with them what looked like a deflated beach ball, with strange markings and the first picture we had seen on this alien world. The picture of a magnificent bird, with its wings stretched wide, as it appeared to land in front of one of the windows. We had to assume that it was some kind of traffic signal that had originally floated somewhere up there but had collapsed on the ground over time. So, our assumption that the locals were avian seemed to be confirmed.

Well, it was time for James and me to be avian as well and I watched him ascend to the lowest of the windows and find his footing on the landing in front. He stood there in the opening and took his time to survey the interior before signaling me to join him. I chose the window next to him and landed, somewhat clumsily, on the ledge in front of it. Out of practice of finding my balance, I guess, but finally, I was stable on my feet and could look inside. It was a cavernous hall with cylindrical walls around it, pierced with the oval-shaped windows that we had seen from outside, all looking down on a platform of some kind, in the center. The platform had a dozen or so spires arranged in concentric circles, surrounding the tallest of them made of some crystalline material, reflecting the rays of light shining on it from all the windows above. Somehow, I had the odd feeling as if I was in some kind of cathedral, waiting for the head priest to start the ceremony. Looking at James in the other window frame, I could see that he had a similar impression because he had put his hands together as if he was praying in a church.

There was nothing else to look at here, so we both descended back to the ground and told the others of what we had seen. We walked around some more among the buildings but couldn't find anything else interesting, so James and I made an attempt to jet up to another window, on a smaller structure, hoping to find a residential unit or some kind of office with more clues as to what the locals looked like and how they lived in the past. James and I split up and entered different buildings to maximize the chance of discovering clues.

The unit I entered on my next try had to be some kind of artist's studio. There was a platform in the middle, with half-finished sculpture-like creations, made from the same crystalline material that we had seen in the 'cathedral' building we had visited before. One entire interior wall was covered with remnants of a giant mural, depicting a lush forest with flying creatures above the trees and that was the first clue I had about what the aliens looked like. They were somewhat bat-like, under both wings they had what looked like arms, ending in six finger-like appendages and an opposable thumb, so they could manipulate objects just like we do with our hands. That explained how they could build an industrial economy.

I was looking for tools that they must have had to create sculptures but found none - the whole room was quite empty apart from the unfinished art pieces as if the owners had packed up everything very carefully before moving somewhere else. After examining a few more empty rooms, I descended to the ground and joined the others. James had a similar impression that the inhabitants packed up all their possessions and abandoned the buildings in the remote past. Was it possible that these aliens were the ancestors of the Minervans? Maybe they had abandoned their planet and moved to the lush and green Minerva. I can't say I blamed them.

Back on our ship, we told everybody what we had found and, of course, the rest of the day was spent in wild speculation about the aliens' past and what might have happened that made them abandon everything and move to a new planet - if they did.

MINERVA

The First Thinker stared at the screen of his Time Scope. He couldn't have any more doubt - the humans arrived at the outer planet and took up orbit around it. That was bad news by itself because the ship was still outside the range of his EM Pulse weapon. He couldn't wait for another planetary meeting to be assembled, he needed a decision and needed it quickly. So, he sent out a mental request to the Great One for a private *meeting as soon as possible. He also contacted the Second and asked him to join the two of them. Now he had to wait for their replies and waiting had never been too easy on him.*

He didn't know what the humans were up to but he feared the worst. Were they planning to establish a base, maybe a military base, on that planet? His Time Scope couldn't read their minds, only show what they were doing. His imagination threatened to run away with him. He alone of his people had been able to decipher the ancestors' writings and from those, he learned about his own race's violent past. If his own people could do so much killing and destruction it should be assumed that all other species were capable of the same and it was his job to protect his people. He was going to convince the Great One and The Second and, if they agreed with him, the rest of the council would follow. The humans must be destroyed.

There was a tiny shadow of a doubt in the back of his mind because the Time Scope also recorded the holographic display outside the human ship, showing images that depicted ordinary, peaceful human life and he assumed that it could be some kind of an attempt at communicating peaceful intentions but in his gut, he knew that humans could not be trusted. It could just be a ploy to deceive. When the existence of his world was at stake, he couldn't take a chance.

His disturbing thoughts were interrupted by a mental request from the Great One to link minds, shortly followed by a similar request from the Second. Contact was established, and their thoughts bounced back and forth between the three of them. Thoughts, as encoded electromagnetic waves, spread at the speed of light and it didn't take long for all the cards to be on the table. During a mind link deception was impossible, their deepest thoughts were wide open for all three to see. The news of the humans in orbit was communicated to the other two, coupled with the *worries of the First Thinker, and his recommendation of destroying the humans. Once all the information had been exchanged, they broke the mental link and agreed to resume after a suitable time for each of them to evaluate the received information and come to a decision. They agreed to abide by the resolution recommended by the majority.*

The Great One was deeply disturbed by the new information she had received. On one hand, she shared the worries presented by The First, on the other hand, she recoiled from his recommendation. Killing sentient beings was against everything she understood about the gods' intentions, she feared that they would be severely punished if they chose that route. What if the First was wrong? What if the humans did have peaceful intentions? How could they live with themselves if they destroyed innocent lives only because they were afraid? If only the humans could respond to the telepathic messages sent to them! Their attempt to project peaceful life outside their ship was observed by the Time Scope but it was only images of their lives, not of their intentions. When the time to reconnect with the other two approached, she knew, without a shadow of a doubt that she would vote against violence. Come what may, she couldn't take the chance of the gods striking them down for genocide. The fate of the humans would have to rest with The Second.

EARTH

Brad Wagoneer, Mayor of Redding, California was desperate. A major Mpox outbreak was sending the town's citizens into the only functioning hospital they still had since the flood during the war that had killed 34,000 people. The hospital was overwhelmed by the influx of feverish people asking for help and it was the mayor's job to find that help somewhere. He had already tried Chico and Yuba City, two of the southern towns, but both had had their electric power cut when Oroville had been burnt out by the wildfire, so his only hope was Sacramento, 160 miles south of them.

The only communication line he had with all the other towns in the valley was the Omega computer which could communicate by radio signals, so he requested his Omega, nicknamed RC to get in touch with Sacramento's Omega. Once the connection was made, he asked to talk to Jonathan, Sacramento's mayor. He outlined Redding's desperate situation and asked if Sacramento could accommodate over a hundred sick people.

Hearing this plea for help, Jonathan felt as if the roof had crashed down on his head because, just a few hours earlier, he had received a similar request from Stockton, their southern neighbor. Due to the town's flooding from the San Joaquin River, the citizens had to be crowded together in all available buildings and the overcrowding condition resulted in the lingering flu-spreading quickly, infecting thousands. Of course, he could not say 'no' to either request but he had no idea where to put all those sick people coming from both directions.

He was realistic enough to know that their life in the Valley was one more crisis away from careening out of control and the only hope they could count on was help from Lifeboat. Now that faster-than-light communication had been established with the ship, they were even more desperate than before to have Lifeboat's crew convince the Minervans that humans were no threat to them. It all depended on one thing: Lifeboat had to find a way to communicate with the telepathic Minervans and that ability depended on the Omegas, working with Chico's University to translate human thought to telepathic EM signals. He got this far in his thinking when he received a signal from SC, indicating an incoming call.

"Jonathan, I am aware of your newest problems, and I may have some good news for you. We successfully analyzed the EM signals recorded by Lifeboat that accompanied the telepathic messages they received from Minerva and now we can create a transmitter/receiver device that can be attached to a human head, enabling the wearer to 'talk' to the aliens telepathically. Of course, we couldn't test it but we are quite confident that it will work, so we transmitted the specs to Lifeboat and they have the tools and the components to create it in the ship's workshop. "

"That's good news indeed, thank you SC for letting me know, but I'm not sure how this will help with our current crises."

"Indeed, this would be a long-term solution, but I have a suggestion for the short term as well."

"Anything I can use right now would be very welcome, SC. Please tell me what you have in mind!"

"You may not know about this, but there was an experimental project before the war to build a hospital in one of California's cave systems, called 'Masonic Caves' 45 miles east of Sacramento along State Route 16. The project was almost completed

when the war broke out, so it is fully equipped to treat up to 500 patients.

"A hospital in a cave? Why on Earth would they want to do that?"

"It had been known for a long time that some caves have a beneficial air quality that helps sick people. The low temperature and high humidity that prevail there have a natural source. These conditions produce clean air without germs, pollen, or fine dust. The cracks and pores in the rock act like a filter for the inflow of air. Any dust or allergen particles present in the air or brought in from outside are enclosed in mist droplets and remain bound to the walls and floor. The cool temperatures and the high humidity ensure that there is a uniform minimum airflow downstream, which additionally cleans the air. Pathogens cannot multiply under these conditions and are eliminated. So, you might be able to send your sick people there if you can restore power, water, and other necessities."

'Wow! What an idea! I never knew that such a project existed right in our backyard. Thanks, SC, I'll investigate immediately. This might just save all those sick people who have nowhere to go."

Jonathan felt as if the roof had just been lifted off his head by the two pieces of good news he received from SC. Now he had a way to deal with the new crisis that had been dropped in his lap. He could hardly wait to tell Octavia that all wasn't lost yet. As if on a clue, she walked into his office, bringing his lunch as usual, so he wasted no time telling her about the two requests he had received that morning from their neighbors in the Valley, as well as SC's news about the cave-hospital they had not known about. The telepathic conversion at this point was a long-term project, still top secret and they just had to wait to find out if Lifeboat could successfully talk to the Minervans. Octavia was smiling from ear to ear, upon hearing this news.

"Isn't this wonderful, Jon, that whenever we think that we can't cope anymore, we somehow always get a lifeline that will carry us over the current crisis?"

"Quite till the next one!" Jonathan couldn't help smiling, seeing Octavia's happy face.

"Seriously, just think how we survived the war and how we managed to get all the help getting rid of Mouch and his cronies. Then the Lifeboat project came along, something we had not even suspected as a possibility, then defeating the Stockton gangsters with more help from Redding, and now a fully equipped hospital had been dropped in our laps. I suspect that if we never give up on life, life will never give up on us."

"You sound very spiritual this morning, Octav, I can use all your faith in providence or whatever it is you believe in."

"It's not providence I believe in, Jon, it's you. You never give up, you investigate every opportunity however remote, and always find a solution. That's one of the things I admire about you."

"Well, as long as we admire each other, all is well. So how is the future mother of my future child today?"

"You should know, you hear me every morning being sick. Whoever said that having a baby is a blessing? It feels more like a curse!"

"I know, sweetheart, and I would help if I could. What I can't understand is why religious people call it intelligent design?"

"OK, smartass, if you were a god, how would you have designed it?"

"Oh, I have plenty of ideas about that."

"Well, educate me, oh you source of all wisdom!"

"OK, you asked for it. For a start, I wouldn't have invented predation. The idea that we must kill other living species to survive feels like cannibalism to me. He already invented photosynthesis for plants so why can't we have photosynthetic skins to absorb energy directly from sunlight? Then, I would have made us lay eggs as dinosaurs did. Instead, you have to push out this gigantic baby from between your legs. It's gross!"

"Thank you, dear god-in-training, for calling me gross!"

"I didn't call you gross, only the design and the process. You are lovely and beautiful, and I hate God for making the process so uncomfortable for you."

"Pssst! Don't anger the creator, we have enough troubles as it goes. We don't need anymore. You know from the bible how vengeful he is."

"I've never read the bible, you know. I started but I got stuck on all the 'begets' at the beginning and I had better things to do. Besides, I was freaked out when I was given a child's version of the bible when I was nine years old, and I saw a picture of Abraham holding a knife to his son's throat to sacrifice him for God."

"I guess that would freak you out, so no more talk about God to spoil the good news we have received today. Do you think that they will be able to talk to the Minervans and convince them that we are no threat?"

"We'll just have to wait to find out. Lifeboat's shuttle should get there in a day or two. I'll pray to the God I hate to keep Lifeboat safe and successful.

"As I said earlier, you investigate every possibility however remote it seems. If praying helps, you'll do it. If it doesn't, I'm sure it won't do any harm."

THE SHIP

We made two more visits to the Gatekeeper planet and both visits yielded the same result. GK planet was a dead world, abandoned eons before by its inhabitants. Countless speculations were floating around about who they were, what happened to them, and where they had gone. We never found any bodies or even skeletons, we had no idea what they looked like. The images of giant birds on the mural in one residence suggested what they might have looked like, and the size of the doors or windows leading into the units suggested the same. The fact that no personal items were found in any of the units we had explored suggested that they had packed up everything in a systematic, organized way and departed to a destination unknown. Could it be that they abandoned their planet to relocate to Minerva? Why would they do that? There was no sign of an invasion that would have forced them to move and no sign of a planet-wide pandemic was seen anywhere. For lack of evidence to the contrary, we assumed that Gatekeeper planet's inhabitants packed up and relocated to a more advantageous planet and the obvious choice would have been the planet next door: Minerva with its benign climate and lush vegetation.

Martha was floating the idea that a climate change of their own forced them to relocate, just as we were trying to do. This assumption was supported by the fact that GK was a dead planet: arid, barren, without any sign of water anywhere. Just like Earth would be in a million years. If this were the case and the Minervans were the descendants of the escaping inhabitants, then chances were that they might be sympathetic to our plight and wouldn't mind offering some help. Anyway, further speculation would have to wait until we had more information.

~~~

Today was a day for celebration. It had started with an announcement from BB, of a breakthrough that we had been unprepared for. As it turned out, our resident genius, the sentient AI quantum computer, had not been idle all these months while we had been hurtling through space at ten times the speed of light. The announcement came during one of our weekly advisory council meetings. During a lull in our conversation, the familiar emotionless voice of our computer spoke up.

"Please excuse the uninvited intrusion into your meeting, but I have to make an announcement that will interest all of you and will have an impact on all your future decisions."

Nobody had an objection to hearing BB out, so he went on after a small pause.

"As soon as the decision to embark on this journey had been made, all the Omegas in the Valley launched a research project to find a way for faster-than-light (FTL) communication. We knew that once Lifeboat left Earth's solar system, you would be cut off from the possibility of consultation with your government in Sacramento. Once FTL travel became possible, FTL communication was a short step forward. We divided the task into two research projects: all the Omegas in the Valley were working on a hyperspace transmitter in the hope that I can develop a receiver using the same principles. It took me longer because I had had no input from the other Omegas, but today I was able to activate it and immediately received a message from Earth that they had been transmitting continuously for two weeks,

waiting for me to have a functional receiver. In their message, I found the specs for the transmitter they had developed, and I had no trouble duplicating it, so now we have two-way communication with Earth, and I am ready to tell you all the news I received from the Valley, as well as broadcast your messages back to Earth."

The stunned silence that followed BB-s announcement lasted no longer than ten seconds, followed by a deafening roar of hurrah and cheering and other spontaneous sounds of approval. The questions thrown at BB from all of us made it impossible to receive the answers in an orderly way but luckily, Captain Farr was very good at maintaining order, so he bellowed at the top of his lungs to silence the unruly scientists.

"Silence, everyone, give the poor computer a chance to tell us the news from Earth without interruption and then ask your questions, one at a time and wait for the answer before asking another. I suggest we go, starting with me (rank has its advantages) in a clockwise order around the table."

Nobody had an objection, so the chattering died down and BB could resume with news from Earth.

We were shocked and saddened by the tragic news of the Oroville wildfire that destroyed most of the town and turned the residents into refugees, most of them escaping to Sacramento. The collateral damage of Yuba City and Chico having to live without the power they had received from Oroville showed how the consequences of climate change could create a domino effect, not leaving any community unscathed. The flooding of Stockton was another consequence that could have been predicted. Our beloved Hopestead, ripped apart by the tornadoes was the first casualty, which still gave us nightmares. All these disasters brought the importance of our mission to the front of our minds and made us feel more determined than ever to succeed. Of all that BB said, the idea of a telepathic helmet the Omegas were working on gave us the greatest thrill. The possibility of two-way communication with the Minervans was the key to any progress we hoped to make in the standoff that held up our mission in an orbit around the Gatekeeper planet. If only we could have that, we could convince them that our plans were peaceful immigration, not something to fear.

Once we discussed all the new information we had from BB, we decided to send a delegation in the shuttle, armed with the telepathic helmet, and head toward the forbidden planet, hoping that the Minervans would let us approach without hostility. We had been projecting our peaceful images non-stop and no new threatening telepathic message was received by Susan while in a state of self-hypnosis. The delegation would outline our peaceful intentions and request that some humans be allowed to immigrate. Minerva was very sparsely populated, one of their continents was completely uninhabited, as far as we could tell, and we would point out the advantages of peaceful inter-species collaboration. If the Minervans were dead set against immigration, we would ask them to allow us to replenish our supplies and continue our journey in search of a habitable planet. Once we had the telepathic helmet, all these issues could be calmly and rationally discussed.

I spent the rest of the day with Martha and Hope, explaining to the little girl that Daddy would be away for a while, but Mummy will stay to make sure Hope behaves herself and doesn't annoy the crew with her incessant questions about everything that little girls shouldn't be curious about. Martha was quite emotional about our separation, the first since we were locked up in separate apartments back in Oroville when our saga started.

"Sweetheart, I understand that you have to go but understanding doesn't make me like it. Just promise me one thing: you take a giant bat-swat with you and if they give you a hard time, teach them a lesson."

"Mommy, what's a bat-swat?" Hope piped up, proving us wrong yet one more time when we thought we were safe from her ever-cocked ears.

"A bat-swat is something, little one, you never want to meet when I am mad at you!" Martha winked at her daughter, turning the whole exchange into a joke as she often did.

That night we made love with unusual intensity as if preparing for those long nights away from each other. We knew what had to be done, we knew the risks and we had made our decisions. Earth had to be saved and finding a new planet where we could start over again was the only solution. Our lives were secondary to the life of the species that had raised us, nurtured us from birth, protected and nourished us and now presented the bill. It was our time to pay the bill. As simple as that.

Little did we know that there was another option.

MINERVA

The Second Thinker knew, without a doubt, that the decision would come down to him. That both excited and scared him at the same time. All his life he had been in the shadow of the First Thinker and now he had a chance to emerge from that shadow and make a mark for himself. In their world, the most important goal for each individual was to gain a reputation and respect for accomplishments. Most tried to achieve it with art and science, but a few ambitious members wanted to be recognized for their wisdom when decisions had to be made about common interests. He knew that The First had not always made the best decisions because he was blinded by fear of the unknown. This fear held them back when opportunities arose for mental and physical evolution. He knew that in the current dilemma, a compromise was needed, something that would minimize the danger while keeping the opportunity open for a meaningful and mutually beneficial relationship with an alien species, for the first time in their history. If only they could establish some form of communication with these humans! In any case, he was going to recommend caution and delay in their reaction to the approaching vessel. In the back of his mind, he was aware of the giant leap in respect, recognition, and esteem he would earn if his advice on delay would prove justified.

After the mind link was re-established, no more discussion was needed. Their thoughts were open and clear, they would wait and hope that some form of dialog could be established with the approaching humans. They broke the link, and each went back to contemplate the possible consequences of their decision.

EARTH

The assertion that the cave hospital was fully equipped was a shameless exaggeration. Indeed, it was originally meant to be fully equipped for up to 500 patients, but that was a long time ago, years before the war. It did have beds but not much else. Jonathan looked at the report he had received the previous day and rubbed his head with both fists, trying to find a way to make it possible to send, and cure, sick people there.

The first problem was access. The cave was high on the mountain at an elevation of 2200 feet and the road leading there was in terrible condition. Due to relentless clear-cutting by an unregulated lumber company, the topsoil had washed down the slopes and the resulting mudslide almost completely buried the road at places. Then the source of electric power that was supposed to service the hospital wasn't there anymore because the hydroelectric power plant had been dismantled and carried off during the war, needed for the war effort. That generator also powered the water pumps that no hospital could operate without. The equipment needed by the doctors and the nursing staff was still in boxes, in unknown condition and the pharmacy still needed to be supplied from somewhere. And the sick people started arriving by bus-loads from both directions.

Jonathan alerted his entire staff to get into emergency mode and do everything possible to restart at a minimal level of functionality as a top priority. His second in command, Rafiq Shlimon had already sent out the construction crew with heavy-duty bulldozers to clear the roads and repair some of the bridges washed out by the downpour that roared down the rocky stream beds. They were followed by a cleaning crew that aired out the caverns and passages and disinfected the wards, also made up the beds with fresh linen acquired from city warehouses.

Jonathan managed to locate the dismantled hydroelectric generators, still unused and stored in boxes, and he sent off a team of engineers and technicians to reinstall the equipment and restore power and water. Finally, he asked for volunteers to provide the necessary human staff for the hospital and was overwhelmed by the response from doctors, nurses, and maintenance workforce who understood the emergency and wanted to do their share. Robotic help was mostly kept in Sacramento, Jonathan didn't want to disrupt their routine operation to create new problems while dealing with his current headache. With this level of feverish activity, it took over a week to get everything ready for the onslaught of sick patients.

It became obvious that the cave hospital didn't have the capacity for all the new arrivals and additional facilities were needed. The first location large enough to handle the number of extra beds was the city library where Carl was running his reading/writing and art workshop for children. Even though it was a service welcomed by the parents, now it proved to be a luxury that they couldn't afford any longer. Carl was told point blank that the space was needed for sick people and that he would be requested to make room for the new beds. To say the least, he wasn't pleased and refused to volunteer for hospital duty. Instead, he requested that he be allowed to continue his art/reading classes in a smaller library. Since it was a much-needed service looking after the children, he was allowed to do so.

Octavia, on the other hand, didn't hesitate for a second and joined the cleaning and maintenance staff to help look after the patients and do whatever was needed. Jonathan was petrified with worry that his pregnant wife was exposed to all those contagious sick people.

"Look at it this way, Jon, I'm worried about you working yourself to death. You don't come home anymore and sleep in your office, so we are even, wasting time and energy worrying about each other. Either we survive this emergency like we did all the others or Lifeboat won't find anyone alive to transport to the shining new planet when they come back. By the way, have you heard from them recently?"

"The latest news is that they had received the specs for the telepathic helmet, built it and now their shuttle is on its way to Minerva. They will attempt to communicate with the natives, using the helmet, and try to convince them that we are no threat. Whatever they can achieve in that regard won't help us in our current situation. The best they can hope for is a long-term solution. In the meantime, we just have to do the best we can."

"Jon, why is it that we have been in constant survival mode, trying to keep our heads above the water? Staggering from one disaster to the other?"

"Count your blessings Octav, at least we don't live on the coast, having to worry about the rising sea level flooding us out. Another perfectly foreseeable consequence of climate change. All we have to worry about are fires, floods, tornadoes, and pandemics. No tsunamis or hurricanes. Aren't we lucky?"

"I know we always cope at the end, but shouldn't all these problems have been expected and prepared for by our leaders?"

"Listen to yourself, sweetheart! What leaders are you talking about? Those who started the war? Or Donald Mouch and his gang who were ripping us off after the war?"

"No, of course not, but we have you now to lead us out of this catastrophe. What I'm wondering about is what happens when you retire. Will the next leader be another Donald or will people finally have learned their lesson and vote for someone who actually wants to help them?"

"I can't think that far ahead sweetheart. For the sake of our child, I hope that the people of Sacramento have learned their lesson and won't let the bastards fool them anymore."

Their speculation about the future and past was interrupted by Rafiq, coming to report on the day's problems and solutions and Octavia knew that their rare moments of intimate discussion were over. She quietly walked out of Jonathan's office to find whatever way she could help with turning the library into another hospital.

THE SHUTTLE

Telepathic communication is the weirdest sensation I have ever experienced. As soon as we received the specs for the telehelmet, as we decided to call it, engineers got busy in the ship's lab and produced two helmets so we could test if it worked. Captain Farr kept one of them (cited rank's privilege again) and I volunteered to test the other. Since no one else was brave enough to fight me for it, I got to be the experimental rabbit. With the specs, we also received instructions on how to use it and what to expect, so I wasn't entirely unprepared. We moved to opposite ends of the shuttle and tried to follow the instructions. We had been told that we shouldn't try to 'talk' or even think in words and sentences because the helmet could only transmit images and emotions and only in the format as if we remembered them.

So, I donned the helmet and tried to think of our mission, how it started, what we wanted to accomplish, and what we were hoping for. That was how we intended to communicate with the Minervans too, so the test served a dual purpose: making sure that the helmet worked and getting ready to present our case to the natives in a way that they would realize that we are no threat to them.

When I finished thinking of our mission and how I felt about it, I tried to empty my mind to get into a receptive mode and that is when the really weird things started. It felt like someone tried to tell me a dream, in a halting way, as when the narrator remembers bits and pieces of the dream with huge gaps in the story, not sure what had happened. It had a familiar taste to it, definitely reminding me of Captain Farr with his decisive, no-nonsense attitude, but with an undercurrent I couldn't recognize, mostly resembling sadness, which was unexpected, considering who was at the other end. I guess it shows that we never quite know each other but, at the same time, I felt embarrassed as if I was invading someone's privacy. I think communicating by telepathy needs practice both in sending and receiving. We were not planning to use it with each other beyond this short experiment but it was important to be prepared when we tried it with the Minervans. If being connected to a familiar human mind felt weird, I could imagine how much weirder it was going to be 'talking' with a totally alien mind.

When James and I finally exchanged impressions about our 'conversation', he surprised me by saying that he had never realized that I had such a powerful personality. What he said was:

"Trevor, your thoughts, memories, and images were so precise, so clear, almost to the point of being pedantic, it felt as if I was listening to one of the Omega computers."

I had to laugh at that because he put his finger on my decades-long experience with programming computers. You can't be imprecise with a computer because it can't guess what you meant to say as we humans do.

After all this, I understood why all the others on the shuttle refused to don the helmet, it must have been fear of opening up one's mind to another person, without knowing what we would reveal about ourselves.

The next experiment we decided on was testing the range of the helmet. We were almost exactly halfway between our ship and Minerva so, if we could reach the ship telepathically, then we should be able to reach the Minervans as well. The engineers had made up one more helmet that was kept on the ship, precisely for this experiment. Someone was wearing this helmet there at a prearranged time, and I was going to try to reach that person with my helmet. I had no idea who it would be, and part of the reason for that was to see if I can recognize someone by his or her thoughts, just as we recognize each other's voices.

So, at the appropriate time, I donned the helmet again, orienting the small parabolic antenna attached to its top in the direction of where the ship was at the moment, and tried to empty my mind to be in a receptive mode, as had been agreed. Almost immediately I felt contact with another mind, proving that the helmet had the range to reach Minerva at least from this halfway point. The feelings and images I was receiving were so familiar, so full of love and fear and hope that I did not doubt that it was Martha at the other end. And then the images started pouring into my mind and that removed any doubt I might have had: I saw little Hope in the bathtub playing with her ducky, I saw our cabin with me floating over the bed, reading something, and, finally, I was receiving sensations so erotic that I felt my face getting hot, hoping that no one around watching me would guess what I was receiving. I was sure it was my Martha deliberately thinking about our last night together just to test my reaction over the helmet. My reaction must have been what she had expected because I definitely 'heard' her laughing at my embarrassment.

Well, the helmet was proven to work and had the necessary range, so it was time to try to contact the Minervans.

MINERVA

The First Thinker was soaring high above the canopy of the jungle, circling over his abode below. He always did that when he had to make an important decision and wasn't sure which way he would go. Flying with his wings stretched wide always relaxed him and gave his mind a reassuring sense of reality. He knew that the action he contemplated would be condemned by his peers because it would be a unilateral action taken against the consensus that they had arrived at during the last mind link, but the stakes were higher than ever before.

He had been watching the humans on his Time Scope almost non-stop during the last three days, observing their visit to the planet they had been orbiting. They used their smaller vessel to send a small group down, spend half a day, and then return to their mother ship. The First had no way of knowing what the purpose of those visits was, probably just a survey visit, but they had found one of the abandoned cities.

And now, a disturbing new development: their smaller vessel left their mother ship and crossed the line toward his home world. They were heading straight toward him, defying the telepathically communicated warning. What was their intention? Did they carry weapons? Was his world under attack?

He recalled, with horror, those images that he had observed before of how a small flying machine had destroyed an entire city on the humans' planet with one terrible weapon that set it all on fire with a gargantuan explosion. If one small ship could do that, there was no telling what their much bigger vessel was capable of.

The humans would be in the range of his EM pulse weapon that he had retrieved from the technology museum, and he was determined to use it, without asking, or telling about it to anyone, and then face the consequences. It was his world too; his way of life and he couldn't risk letting the humans destroy it.

It was time to return, land, and prepare. He had read the instructions and it was easy and simple to use it. Once it acquired the target, all he would need to do was to wait until it was fully charged and then trigger the pulse. He could observe with the time scope to see what happened. The weapon would not destroy the human vessel, only disable all its electrical circuits, together with all synaptic activity in the brains of its crew. It would continue drifting toward homeworld and probably burn up in the atmosphere when it reached its destination. Nobody would need to know what happened to it, probably no one would know that it was even there. The humans in their main vessel would not know what disabled their scout ship. They most probably wouldn't try it again and, hopefully, would just go away, back to where they had come from. Decision made, he descended to the ground and started his preparations.

~~~

The Great One had a strange sensation she had never experienced before. It felt like remembering something that she ought to do but somehow had forgotten what it was. It also felt like trying to recall a memory that lingered on the edge of her consciousness, flitting away when she tried to get hold of it. It eluded every effort she made to bring it to the surface of her awareness and that frustrated her because she was proud of her mental acuity. She decided to induce a tele-hypnotic state that would clear the cobweb in her mind in no time. Once she acquired that higher level of consciousness, she had the shock of her life: what she had felt was a telepathic tendril coming from a mind he couldn't recognize. She knew exactly how any mind of her own species would feel with a sweet familiarity, but this thought wave was completely new to her. It had to come from off-planet and the only source she could think of was the human vessel. Have the humans developed an ability to communicate with her people? Were they trying to tell her something?

She purposefully relaxed her mind to make it as receptive as possible so the jumble of mental tendrils would coalesce and firm up into intelligent thought. She half succeeded because it wasn't thoughts that she received but images and emotions that she was familiar with. The emotions were the easiest to identify and she immediately recognized sadness, hope, desire for friendship, fear, and determination. The images belonged to an alien world, showing a strange species as they were running away from ferocious atmospheric blasts that ripped their buildings apart, clambering onto a cylindrical machine of some kind and shooting up into the air, leaving their planet behind.

The emotions she received were so intense that she severed the mental connection to regain her balance. She had to analyze this strange communication - if that's what it was. It took her a while but eventually, she managed to condense the images and emotions into a coherent message. The humans were escaping their planet, looking for a new home and hoping that they would find help from her species. The feeling of sadness, fear, hope and most of all, open benevolence were unmistakable. They were no threat; they were helpless refugees from the same fate that her ancestors had had to avoid by abandoning the ancestral planet in the remote past.

She had to contact the First Thinker immediately before he would do something unforgivable. For some time now she had received very disturbing vibrations from the First, every time they met, and she suspected that his single-minded obsession with, and fear of, the humans would push him into an unthinkable breach of their most basic social rule: no one takes unilateral action against the consensus of the entire council.

The Great One sent out an urgent mental call to alert the council for immediate group-think, as well as a stop-and-desist order to the First One, should he be willing to take unauthorized action.

Then, she had to wait and hope that she wasn't too late.

~~~

The First Thinker was ready to fire his EM pulse weapon when he received the order from the Great One. He was tempted for a few heartbeats to defy the order and face the consequences, but to go against a direct Stop and Desist order, coming from the Great One was too much of a risk to take. The secrecy of what happened to the humans would be gone, The Great One would demand a mind link and he couldn't hide what he had done. She would make it public, and the humiliation was too great to contemplate. He would become a pariah and would lose his standing in the Council as the First Thinker. With great reluctance, he withdrew his hand from the weapon's trigger and locked it into safe mode.

He had to go to the meeting the Great One called, but he didn't want to go there without a plan. He still wanted to save his planet from the human invasion he was sure was coming and, if he wasn't allowed to destroy their scout ship, he would have to make sure that the humans lost their reason to come. There was only one way he could think of to accomplish that. He would have to help the humans to repair their planet so they wouldn't have to leave it.

In the Tech Museum that he often visited he remembered seeing some big round tanks with translucent walls that had some strange iridescent swirling appear inside when he tried to move them. He wondered enough to investigate further and deciphered the writing on the label that accompanied every item in the Museum. To his great surprise, he learned that the objects were pressure tanks that contained the gas his ancestors had developed to remove carbon from the CO_2 in the atmosphere and thus reverse the deadly climate change that was fast making their planet unlivable. In the end, they abandoned the idea of using it because by that time their planet was so far gone that it was doubtful that the remedy would come in time to save them, so they decided to emigrate to the next planet that was in pristine condition. They would give up technology so their new planet wouldn't suffer the same fate but take samples of all they had developed and store them in a hidden museum just in case they ever would need technology again. He would go to the council meeting and recommend letting the humans have these tanks so they could save their own planet and never come back here again.

EARTH

Carl Armstrong was pissed off. He had actually started enjoying his reading/writing/art workshop with the children when he was booted out of the Main Library and shoehorned into a much smaller and much less adequate facility. How was he supposed to keep up the same level of artistic presentations without proper equipment that he didn't have anymore? Don't the dunderheads get it? Life without art is not worth living. Sick people will survive somehow but Culture is fragile and needs care and nourishment.

Talking about nourishment, where was his breakfast? He was used to getting the regular food deliveries that Jonathan had promised and, since they had been exiled to this new dump, nothing anymore. How was he supposed to deal with hungry children? Never mind his own stomach growling. He remembered that he had a fully stocked cupboard and fridge in the Main Library and all that food belonged to him and the children, so he was going to get it back. Hopefully, he thought, it will last until the bureaucrats sorted it all out.

He told the children to get on with their last assignment and headed over to the Main Library, intent on demanding his supplies. When he got there, he didn't recognize the place. All the bookshelves were pushed against the walls, making the books completely inaccessible. The entire floor space was covered with beds, jammed together so tight that there was hardly any room in between them. The beds were mostly occupied by moaning and miserable-looking sick people and the rest of the floor was taken up by doctors and nurses rushing about, from bed to bed, distributing food, drinks, and medicine. There was no sign of his fridge and cupboard with his badly needed food.

He looked around, trying to find someone in charge, so he could present his demands. To his surprise, the first familiar face he saw was the mayor's wife, scurrying from bed to bed, obviously pregnant when he took a closer look. The second familiar face was Dr. Stromberg, the holier-than-thou psychiatrist who had tried to talk him into volunteering for slave labor. Carl marched up to him in a determined way to demand his food stock but had to run after him as the doctor hurried away, carrying a bucket. When he caught up with him, he realized that the bucket was full of stinking waste, so he wrinkled his nose and stayed a few feet away.

"Oh, it's you, Carl, happy that you came to help. Please empty this bucket into the toilet and then come back for more. We can use all the help we find."

"Dr. Stromberg, I came to retrieve that food stack I had here before we were forced out. The children need their daily snack, or they lose concentration in doing their assignments."

Sidney looked at him as if he had dropped down from the sky. He found it hard to believe that any human being can be that indifferent to all the suffering around him.

"Carl, I have no time for this. If you don't want to help, then get the hell out of here. You are obstructing traffic."

With that last word, he turned away and hurried off to empty the bucket he was holding.

Carl was speechless. Urbane, polite, professional Dr. Stromberg had become a rude orderly in a stinking hospital, carrying shit buckets. He was not going to find sympathy, let alone help here, so he walked out of that horrible place back to his clean and comfortable new library. He was still hungry but at least he was surrounded by beauty and culture here. He walked around the room, looking at the progress his pupils had made and nodded with satisfaction. That's where he belonged.

It was late the next afternoon when he started feeling nauseous, with his throat scratchy and his forehead feeling hot. He couldn't believe it, he had been in that stinking library for only a few minutes and he must have caught something. Well, he needed help, quickly, so he went to his usual hospital, only to be turned away. The triage nurse told him that the hospital was full beyond capacity, and he should either go with the next transport to the cave hospital or go back to the main library where they still had some empty beds. He was not going to humiliate himself by going back there, so Dr. Stromberg could gloat. He decided to wait for the next transport going up the mountain. Since it was almost an hour's drive away, he was sure most sick people wouldn't want to be so far from their homes and families, so chances were that the cave hospital would be less busy and less crowded.

When he finally arrived, with a bus full of sick
people, he found it difficult to believe that anyone
could squeeze a hospital into that cave. He had
difficulty entering the cave and then following
winding passages, walking on sandy ground, looking
at the walls of the cave barely illuminated by hastily
strung up electric wires, connecting haphazardly
placed lanterns. After about a hundred feet of that,
the cave walls receded, opening up a spacious cavern,
the floor of which was covered by hundreds of beds
tightly jammed together, just like in the library. As
far as he could tell in the dim light, the passage he
had entered from continued on the other end of the
cavern, presumably leading to other wards where the
cave opened up again to a suitable cavern.

The triage nurse who had been leading his group
from the entrance took his temperature, asked for his
symptoms, and then led him to a still empty bed
where he was told to put on a gown after stashing his
clothes away in a cardboard box under the bed. He
did what he was told and happily lay down on the bed
which wasn't the most comfortable bed he had ever
encountered, but by this time his fever had made him
so groggy that he couldn't care less about the bumps
in the mattress.

Carl spent the next week in that bed, being looked
after mostly by volunteers who walked from bed to
bed, dispensing food, drinks, and medications. The
first three days were the worst when he was mostly

unaware of what was going on around him, he was fighting demons in his feverish state. One of the demons looked like Dr. Stromberg. He was arguing with the doctor, still trying to convince Stromberg that he owed nothing to society, the people helping him were all volunteers, and he had never asked them to be there.

Sydney Stromberg didn't argue back, just stood there looking into his soul and he hated him for that. Didn't the damn doctor realize that Carl represented the noblest part of humanity, the Culture that elevated their grubby lives into a realm that made life worth living? He remembered an argument Sydney had given him about how a house without the supporting structures being sound and working properly, was no good, no matter how tastefully it was decorated. He also remembered his own argument about how a house was defined by its contents and not by the roof and the four walls. And then Sydney mercilessly told him that all the furniture would be useless if the roof was leaking, or the walls caved in.

"Carl, culture is fine as it goes, but you depend on the engineers, doctors, and workers and not the other way around. You and your culture are only a luxury if we can afford you. You owe a lot to these people who keep you alive. There is only one sin that comes close to the sin of biting the hand that feeds you: and it is the sin of not saying thank you and then passing on the help you received to others when you have the opportunity."

He still remembered Sydney's stern face as he had been lecturing him on who owed whom what, three days later when he was discharged from the hospital and bumped around on the bus on the long drive back to town. His first trip took him to the Main Library where he told the triage nurse that he was volunteering to help with whatever they needed.

SHUTTLE

Finally, we arrived and took up orbit around Minerva. Nobody tried to shoot us down, not even a telepathic threat. Both I and Captain Farr wore our helmets at all times, waiting for reactions from the Minervans. They must have noticed our arrival, probably debating what to do about us. We didn't attempt to land but rather waited for an invitation and directions.

We now had a good look at their planet from our shuttle. They have two large bodies of water, I would call them oceans, separating the landmass into two oddly shaped continents between them. There is another good-sized land mass rising out of one of the oceans. I wouldn't call it a continent, I'd rather call it an island with what looked like an extinct volcano in the middle.

One of the continents is almost entirely covered with lush forest, bisected by a wide and winding river flowing from a mountain range into the ocean. We could not detect any towns or even smaller settlements, the Minervans must live close to the ground, their structures obscured by the giant trees growing everywhere.

No sign of industry, mining, factories, let alone space-, or even airports. More and more it looked like the Minervans were a pre-industrial, probably agrarian society. They might even be hunter-gatherers living off the land. Then how could they imagine they could destroy our ship? Maybe it was just an empty threat? We'll have to wait to find out. The disturbing thought I had was that they must have had some concepts of space travel, spaceships, and explosions and they were able to detect us approaching the Gatekeeper planet so they had to have some astronomy with telescopes or other instruments. If they did, where had it come from? Could it be that they did have some technology while living on GateKeeper and brought it with them when they migrated here? If they did migrate here. So many unanswered questions and we had to wait for the answers.

As we were orbiting the planet, we kept altering our orbit, so at each pass, we could see yet unseen part of the landscape below, hoping to discover the main center of their civilization, if it did exist, but so far all we had seen was land and water.

After a day with no contact from the planet, we decided to start broadcasting with our helmets and ask them to allow us to land at any location of their choosing. It was hard to communicate without a common language, but we just kept imagining our shuttle landing at various places and waited for some kind of reaction.

Finally, after we had completed more than a dozen orbits, my helmet suddenly blasted a message into my brain. The intensity and the volume of that blast almost knocked me off my feet, so I quickly adjusted the volume of the reception circuit, so I could properly understand what the message was about.

It was a very short and simple instruction, that showed our shuttle landing on that big island, at the foot of that volcano, on a good-sized clearing in the surrounding woods. The emotional content of the message mostly felt like a stern warning, which I interpreted as an order not to deviate from our designated landing spot. The message was repeated several times, each followed by a pause as if waiting for acknowledgment, so I composed a thought in my mind and projected the imagined landing of our shuttle as instructed. I repeated it several times and, finally, the communication was over. The Minervans were waiting to see us land as we agreed.

~~~

We, or rather Captain Farr, managed to land on the clearing without any trouble. According to our agreement, I would be the only one to exit the shuttle and wait for contact, the rest of the crew would stay inside, ready to take off at the first sign of trouble. This was the fourth time since leaving Earth that I attempted to stand up and walk and I have to admit I was grateful for the planet's low gravity. Despite the vigorous exercise routine that I had followed on both the ship and the shuttle, my leg muscles were not as they used to be.

After I stepped outside the airlock, I took a tentative short breath from the unaccustomed air and found it agreeable if a bit too cold. I was alone, and nobody waited for me, so I walked around the shuttle, looking for clues as to what was supposed to happen. The grass under my feet was slightly wet, not growing higher than mid-calf, and liberally sprinkled with pink and blue flowers. It all felt very pleasant, and I could imagine myself living there if we were allowed.

Soon I realized that I wasn't alone anymore because, looking up, I saw three magnificent giant birds circling for a landing. They looked like bats with green leathery wings, sparsely covered with fur - two of them with green but the third one with pure white fur. They landed a few feet away from me and I felt dwarfed in their midst, they were towering over me by two feet or more.

We had a good look at each other as I was finally face-to-face with native Minervans. They had the strangest faces I had ever seen. I had expected beaks, but they had a mouth instead. Two small eyes under bushy eyebrows and a couple of round ears on top of huge heads. Under their wings, they had two powerful-looking arms ending with almost human-like hands with six digits and what looked like a thumb. They were standing on two remarkably bird-like feet ending in three clawed digits.

I have no idea what their impression of me was, but I had no time to find out because the one in the middle, with the white fur, suddenly stepped up close to me, and looked intently into my eyes. I resisted the urge to run back inside the shuttle and stood my ground on slightly wobbling knees. I stood motionless while the big white Minervan gently removed my helmet and held my head between its powerful hands. Then the strangest sensation I had ever had took hold of me, suddenly I felt my mind open up like a book and I was powerless to stop **it** from examining my brain neuron by neuron, it seemed.

Time stopped for me, and I just stood there, waiting for **it** to end.

When it did, I was in control of myself once more and reached out for the helmet, so I could try to communicate with them, but it turned out I didn't need **it** anymore. During the examination of my mind, the creature must have implanted a message into my brain. **It** was not a message in words and sentences but had the effect of flashes of memories and instant knowledge, like something I had known all my life.

It was the knowledge of how its species had a technology that almost destroyed them, to the point where they had to abandon their ancestral planet when it became unlivable. It was the knowledge of their present peaceful, close to the earth living and also **its** knowledge of our desperate situation on our Earth and our quest for a new homeland. Finally, **it** was the knowledge that under no circumstances would we be allowed to immigrate to their home world, but we could find a compatible planet at the coordinates they were going to supply. Similar size, therefore, gravity, and a similar atmosphere. Mostly covered by vegetation but no wildlife yet. They had considered it for migration when they had to abandon their planet but decided to stay in their own solar system. This new planet was half the distance from our Earth, in the almost opposite direction. The galactic coordinates appeared in my mind, and I knew I would never forget them.

The last piece of knowledge I was given was that once we left to rejoin our ship, no human would be allowed, under any circumstances, to come near their world again. They had enough technology left to destroy us if we ignored their warning and they wouldn't hesitate to use it.

Once the white one recognized that its message was delivered into my brain, without further ado it launched itself into the air, closely followed by the other two. After a few spiraling circles, they gained altitude and flew off toward the mainland.

~~~

Once the three large Minervans were gone I was joined by the whole crew who gathered around me, all wanting to know what had happened. I told them as concisely as I could, still recovering from the experience myself.

The big question now was: what to do next? The Minervans wanted us gone and flatly refused to let humans move to their planet. We had two choices: either go straight back to Earth or continue our journey to the coordinates I was given and satisfy ourselves that it had the best chance of supporting life and was also uninhabited. Problem was that we had enough food and fuel to make it back to Earth but, if we continued in the opposite direction, we would gamble on being able to replenish both food and fuel before we returned home. So, the decision was made: back to our ship and then take off for home. Of course, we would have to consult with our government in Sacramento, let them know what the situation was, and make sure that they would approve our decision.

We were sure they would because that was the safest and the most logical thing to do.

MINERVA

The First Thinker and the Great One were linking minds one last time while watching the humans leave their solar system. While linking minds there are no secrets, all their thoughts, feelings, and all their memories are wide open for both to see and, therefore, very seldom used. However, considering the seriousness of the current crises, they needed to know each others' perceptions of the recent events and their significance.

The Great One became aware of how close the First had come to destroy the human ship, due to his fear of invasion and the destruction of his people. Knowing that his motives were noble, she understood and forgave him for the temptation to disobey their most sacred rule: nobody breaks decisions arrived at by consensus.

The First, on the other hand, became aware of the new and rich understanding the Great One acquired by linking minds with one human. She had become aware of the complex and painfully contradictory mind of another sentient being who harbored the widest range of emotions she had ever witnessed in a mind. She was saddened by the pain and desperate disappointment this human mind felt about its own species for the terrible history of mass murder and destruction over the centuries, caused by the irrational fear and hate of their leaders. She also became aware of its deep love for its mate, its child, and all the other humans it had been calling friends. And, finally, she learned about their desperate need to save their planet and she had seen signs of trust in their surviving community after the deadly war that had destroyed most of its world. Finally, she became aware of the overwhelming emotion of hope all these humans felt in their struggle to survive and start again with their newly learned lesson: the valley they lived in would be a valley of hope for a better world.

The last, hesitant thought the First Thinker felt in the Great One's mind was: "maybe we could have offered them the western continent. It's uninhabited and we have no plans to move there. Hardly any trees which we need, but it could have been a perfect agricultural land where they could grow their food."

The responding thought in the First One's mind was: "You don't know them as well as I do. You have observed one human's mind, but I have studied them for years. Their violent ways are beyond anything we could have imagined, and they cannot be trusted."

After sharing thoughts and feelings about these humans, The First and The Great One agreed that they had made the right decision by letting them leave unharmed and helping them to find a new planet. This was the first time in known history that their species encountered aliens and they agreed that thorough and deep analysis was required to draw the right conclusions for the next time, should this ever happen again. A consensus was reached and their respect for each other was restored.

EARTH

JOnathan was beyond exhaustion. These had been the hardest six months he remembered. The pandemic was over, not because the patients were all cured but because those they couldn't help died. The hospitals they had set up served only one useful purpose: to prevent the disease from spreading to the general population. It was contained in these three locations, and it had burned itself out. It had taken very hard work and merciless control to prevent an outbreak outside the hospitals and it had taken a lot out of Jonathan and all the people helping him. His biggest fear of Octavia catching one of the diseases never turned into a real threat: she was young, healthy, and had high resistance despite the tireless effort she had made in helping the sick. *"If I were religious, I would thank God for that."* he thought and allowed a secret little smile to creep up on his face.

And now, that the pandemic was over, he had one bright light of hope shining on his mind: Lifeboat was returning from its year-long scouting mission. They hadn't found a new planet for humanity and the only one that could have been suitable was populated by sentient giant bats who didn't want to share their world with humans but offered them some help that would, hopefully, lead to finding a new home safe to migrate to.

It was at that point of thinking that he received the news that Lifeboat had been spotted approaching Earth, just outside the Moon's orbit. It would take a day or two for it to land and he could hardly wait to see his friends again.

~~~

We were finally home, our Lifeboat in geosynchronous orbit over Sacramento and it will stay there until we need it again on our final departure to the new planet. The whole group of our advisory council, plus our families were the first to take the shuttle down to Earth. From space, we had observed the ravages climate change had done to the planet, with Florida and the coastal cities underwater, huge areas of the Midwest turned to desert, and no sign of the polar ice caps, we were almost afraid to step outside after we had landed. When we did, the tropically hot and humid air hit us in the face and breathing was difficult. After a whole year spent, with very brief interruptions in a weightless condition, standing up in one Earth gravity was brutal on all of us, despite the vigorous exercise schedule we had maintained on Lifeboat, plus the electrochemical muscle stimulation we received from our medical staff once a week. Still, being back on the ground was a thrilling if somewhat bittersweet feeling.

We were ushered into a waiting bus that took us through the lifeless city to the entrance of the biggest underground shopping mall we remembered from before the war. Through the deserted streets we couldn't even see a dog, let alone people walking about. Once we were underground, our bus took us to a parking place where we could disembark and take our first look at the new city we had never seen.

It was a sight to behold. Our guide told us that we were on the top level of a five-level structure. We remembered the skylights overhead and the walkways between stores that had offered all kinds of goods to those inclined to spend their money on things they didn't really need. Now we could see no displays in the windows, they were mostly curtained or showed various offices inside. We were told that this level harbored the residential units for claustrophobic people who needed the natural light coming through the skylights. It was also used for the various offices required by the administration workers who were running the city with its many needs for food production and distribution, maintenance of the energy units, sanitation and ventilation, health care, and education facilities. The lower three levels were subdivided and furnished for over 30,000 residential family units, serviced by communal kitchens and bathrooms, where we would be assigned lodging ourselves if we decided to stay. The lowest level was devoted to food factories, hydroponics, and other manufacturing facilities that the city depended on, as well as the fusion generator and the geothermal power plant.

The air was maintained at a comfortable level of temperature and humidity, so unlike the steam bath, we had to walk through from the shuttle to the bus. While our guide explained all this to me, I couldn't stop being amazed at the magnitude of this gigantic accomplishment the people of Sacramento had managed to complete in a little over a year, despite the pandemic they had to deal with. When we finally arrived at the administrative center, we walked into a large conference room, and finally, we met old friends. Jonathan and Octavia greeted us with hugs and led us to comfortable chairs that we were very eager to sink into. Earth's gravity had almost proved too much for us by the time we arrived.

When everyone was seated, Jonathan officially greeted us and asked for a verbal report on our journey. They had already read the written report we had sent down from Lifeboat as soon as we had arrived in our solar system but now he wanted us to fill in the details with our personal views and impressions.

"Trevor, my first question is for you: can we trust the Minervans about that planet they suggested for colonization? I understand why you couldn't go there to check it out for yourself but now we have to depend on the say-so of a not-entirely-friendly alien species. Is it possible that they lied or exaggerated just to get rid of you?"

That question surprised me because it had never occurred to me to doubt the sincerity of the Minervans. I had never been in a mind-link with another sentient being before but just as I knew that my mind was an open book during the exchange, unable to keep secrets or hidden thoughts, I was absolutely sure that it was a necessary mutual condition for the mind link to be possible at all. I told Jonathan all this and I could see he found it hard to take it all in.

"OK, Trevor, I have to depend on your assessment and we will plan accordingly. Not everybody wants to emigrate, of course, just as not everybody wants to live underground either. There are a lot of citizens who refuse to leave their homes and will do whatever they can to isolate themselves from the heat and the weather conditions. We also have citizens who think that living in a clean, modern, high-tech community such as we have here is the best way for 22nd-Century civilized human beings. They laud the close-knit community that such an environment encourages, with many artistic and cultural opportunities, both active and passive. Our resident artist and author, Carl Armstrong is running educational workshops in the central library that was also moved underground and he swears he would never want to live any other way. On the other hand, some of us can hardly wait to move to an unspoiled planet and have a fresh start, escaping the ugly consequences of our past sins that caused climate change."

"Some of *us?*" I couldn't help blurting **it** out.

"Yes, Trevor, Octavia, and I decided to join you when you leave again. She is severely claustrophobic which prevents her from living in the city, and she wants a fresh start for our family that includes me and our baby boy."

"Wow! That's a surprise, I always thought that you and Sacramento were inseparable."

"I must admit, I'll leave with a heavy heart but for me, Octavia's happiness trumps any other consideration. Besides, this could be an adventure and you may need another philosophical administrator."

"Well, for us it's good news, and welcome to the team. Now that the decision is made, we'll have to make very careful plans to prepare for this journey. Our BB told us that all the Omegas have been working with Chris and the scientists at Chico University and managed to increase the efficiency of our Alcubierre space drive so it can now achieve 30 times the speed of light, so our traveling time can be cut down to a third of what it was before. Just as well because the new planet is farther away, and sustained weightlessness is pretty hard on everybody."

"OK, Trevor, I suggest that we leave it at that, and you guys can retire in the units assigned to you and have a well-deserved rest. Someone will show you the nearest kitchen and bathroom facilities for your use. Tomorrow we can start serious planning"

EPILOGUE

It took us over a month to get ready for our second departure. The longest part of the preparation was, of course, rebuilding our hyperdrive, so our speed could triple and thus cut-down on our travel time. Would we succeed or would we make the same mistakes that had plagued us for millennium? I was optimistic about the future. It's a brand-new world, with no natives, no wildlife, and nothing to fight over. We have already worked out the basic principles of our society and by eliminating money from the picture we had established social justice where everyone's basic needs were guaranteed while giving scope for individual freedom. The hundred human beings carried by our ship were all eager to start a productive life and, with hard work, create a new start for the human race. We would be followed by many other migrants; our Lifeboat was going to shuttle back and forth with loads of eager immigrants all looking for a clean and prosperous life.

One disturbing question lurking in the back of my mind was: are we genetically predestined to establish domination structures where one or more person needs to push weaker people around and tell them how to live their lives? That remains to be seen and history is not very encouraging in that regard. However, the multiple disasters of the last few years should have given us a stern warning: Screw up this last chance and we are done - our species proved itself inviable, ready for extinction.

As I looked at the view screen, showing the fast-disappearing blue and white globe of our birthplace, I wondered how innocent and peaceful it looked from out here. Also, how fragile. When it finally shrank to a tiny blue dot, I had to think of a passage from an Earth scientist a hundred years in the past, who wrote the following in his book when an Earth satellite, Voyager 1, on 14 February 1990, was about 6.4 billion kilometers away. Caught in the center of scattered light rays Earth appears as a tiny point of light, a crescent only 0.12 pixel in size.

"Look again at that dot. That's here. That's home. That's us. On it everyone you love, everyone you know, everyone you ever heard of, every human being who ever was, lived out their lives. The aggregate of our joy and suffering, thousands of confident religions, ideologies, and economic doctrines, every hunter and forager, every hero and coward, every creator and destroyer of civilization, every king and peasant, every young couple in love, every mother and father, hopeful child, inventor and explorer, every teacher of morals, every corrupt politician, every "superstar," every "supreme leader," every saint and sinner in the history of our species lived there--on a mote of dust suspended in a sunbeam.

The Earth is a very small stage in a vast cosmic arena. Think of the rivers of blood spilled by all those generals and emperors so that, in glory and triumph, they could become the momentary masters of a fraction of a dot. Think of the endless cruelties visited by the inhabitants of one corner of this pixel on the scarcely distinguishable inhabitants of some other corner, how frequent their misunderstandings, how eager they are to kill one another, how fervent their hatreds.

Our posturings, our imagined self-importance, the delusion that we have some privileged position in the Universe, are challenged by this point of pale light. Our planet is a lonely speck in the great enveloping cosmic dark. In our obscurity, in all this vastness, there is no hint that help will come from elsewhere to save us from ourselves.."

— Carl Sagan, *Pale Blue Dot*, 1994"

The End

Other books by the author

- The Prism of my Mind – Poems
- Humane Physics– Classical Physics
- House Arrest – a Story of Liberation –
- Meandering – Short Story collection
- A Dark end Stormy Knight – Fantasy
- Saved in Time – An Escape Story – novel
- Epicycle Physics – Modern Physics
- Humane Physics – The Whole Story
- Opposing Forces – a Memoir
- Perembulations _ Musings of an Old Man
- Rainbow Valley A Story of Choices
-

About the author

Francis Mont has been living in Canada for the past 49 years after he emigrated from his native Hungary where he studied science and received a degree in Theoretical Physics. Over the years he did research, application, and teaching in Mathematics, Physics, and Computer Science. He is interested in profound questions, both in science and in social philosophy. He is a 'big picture' person, focusing on fundamental principles and the defining essence of the topic at hand. He also pursues independence and self-reliance to the best of his abilities, as his solar power system and year-round greenhouse demonstrate. He writes poetry, plays classical violin, dabbles at wood carving, and has not yet stopped building the house he and his wife and (currently) five cats live in.

Ordering Information

You can order a copy of this book at the following venues:

- www.alibris.com
- www.biblio.com
- www.montland.ca

or by sending email to the author to the following address: francis@montland.ca

I will respond to queries within 24 hours.